A
LETTER
FROM
Munich

A JACK BAILEY NOVEL

MEG LELVIS

Black Rose Writing | Texas

ISBN: 978-1-68433-447-6
PUBLISHED BY BLACK ROSE WRITING
www.blackrosewriting.com

Printed in the United States of America
Suggested Retail Price (SRP) $16.95

A Letter from Munich is printed in Book Antiqua

*As a planet-friendly publisher, Black Rose Writing does its best to eliminate unnecessary waste to reduce paper usage and energy costs, while never compromising the reading experience. As a result, the final word count vs. page count may not meet common expectations.the reading experience. As a result, the final word count vs. page count may not meet common expectations.

For my sister, *Carole*
&
In loving memory of our mother, *Renate*

Acknowledgments

Special Thanks to:

Reagan Rothe and his staff at *Black Rose Writing*
David King, Design Director at *Black Rose Writing*
Mark Pople, Editor
Danielle Hartman Acee, Tech Assistant

Houston Writers critique friends: Roger Paulding, Lynne Gregg,
Jim Murtha, Carolyn Thorman, Bill Ottinger, Barbara Andrews,
Fern Brady, Landy Reed, Connie Gillen, Raul Herrera
& Melanie Ormand

As always, Carole and Myrna
Susanne Wagner for help with German usage

My family, Gary, Kristy, Rebecca, Cate, Nolan, and Teddy

Also, many thanks to my relatives in Bavaria who inspired
some of the characters in this book.

Further resources:

MacDonough, Giles. *After the Reich*. Basic Books, 2007.
Sunstein, Cass R. "It Can Happen Here." *The New York Review* 28
June 2018: pp.64-65. Print.
Munich Documentation Center for the History of National
Socialism. Munich, Germany.

A

LETTER

FROM

Munich

A JACK BAILEY NOVEL

OTHER BOOKS BY MEG LELVIS:

BAILEY'S LAW

BLIND EYE

More than kisses letters mingle souls.
~John Donne~

Letters are among the most significant memorial
a person can leave behind them.
~Johann Wolfgang von Goethe~

TODAY

Without the letter they never would have known. The letter discovered by accident. Or was it meant to be found?

Addressed to their father, delicate vellum, crinkled, musty. Postmarked München 14.7.46. Stuffed in the frayed cardboard box, hidden within long-forgotten war relics. Did he forget to destroy it so many years ago?

Pale blue, nearly white, scalloped edges, translucent. Flowery script with sufficient English words so he could understand.

Who can answer the questions of fairness, decency, good faith? Better to unravel the truth and hurt some? Or lock the truth in your soul and deny others a right to know?

Then again……. 'No legacy is so rich as honesty.'

And it was all about the legacy, wasn't it?

Germany, 1930s

The horror crept toward us slowly, stealthily. Unnoticed, it emerged through shadows of green forests, lakes, even lilacs. Soon it transformed from beauty, health, strength, power. Campfires, songs, but most of all pride. Only Papa knew. He knew, and it cost him his life

At first our awareness began with him. Then our friends. Then the schools. Then the girls camp. We lived under a deepening shadow. But we didn't know.

We were the Schröders, an ordinary German family, two boys, two girls, Papa a dentist. We lived near Munich in the peaceful village of Dachau.

Flowers bloomed in every yard on our street. Oh, the blue cornflowers were exquisite. And the lilacs. Their perfume filled the air.

•   •   •   •   •

I am Renate. I was only five when it began. My best friend, Judith, lived down the block in a big two-story home. We played with our dolls, went on picnics, swam, and rowed in her father's boat on Karlsfelder See. Her dolls were nicer than mine. My sister, Ariana and I had one Kestner porcelain doll. Judith had five.

Judith's father was our doctor until one day Papa said we had to find a new one. *But why can't we keep going to Dr. Friedman?* Papa didn't answer. After that we had to go to Dr. Schmidt, whose office was farther away past our school and across Meer bridge. But we still played with Judith, so I didn't think much about it.

Until later.

CHAPTER 1
Munich, June 2012

Jack Bailey did not believe in fate, but the invitation to visit Germany could be an omen. A silent voice niggled at his brain. *You must investigate the letter.* The letter he thought would remain a secret he and his brother would take to their grave.

He arrived in Munich with his friend, Karl Scherkenbach, nicknamed Sherk, whose extended family lived in the area. Jack had jumped at the chance to accompany him on his yearly trip overseas to visit his relatives. He would tell Sherk the real reason later.

The next evening, Jack had recovered from jet lag and was settling in for the night. Cool summer air floated through an open window of the comfortable guest room in Sherk's family vacation home. After he popped a couple Ambien to avoid insomnia that plagued him for years, he lay on the bed's overly firm mattress staring at stark white walls offset by two Georgia O'Keeffe-type large prints of purple and yellow flowers. Colors blurred as he let his thoughts drift back in time.

•   •   •   •   •

Two months ago, Jack had abruptly quit his job as a detective with Chicago's Police Department, after coping with a difficult sergeant and frustrating, never-ending bureaucracy. However, he could well afford the Germany trip, thanks to a recent windfall from his former father-in-law's estate. Do him good to get away. Besides, Sherk had been his loyal partner in the department for two years, a burden not everyone could bear. Jack, described by many as a rugged Liam Neeson look-alike, had not mellowed with age. He'd often overheard co-workers mumbling to Sherk. *Don't know how you put up with Bailey, man.*

Last month Jack phoned his older brother, Tommy. "I'm going to Munich with Sherk. We leave in June for a couple weeks."

Tommy had nodded, paused. "You gotta do it, Jack. As long as you'll be in Munich, take the letter. It may be our only chance."

Now the time had come. He was counting on Sherk's fluent German to help unravel the decades-old question posed in the letter. But he'd have to tell him about it first.

CHAPTER 2

The next day Jack was ready to meet Sherk's grandparents. His curiosity had piqued when Sherk told him about his grandfather, a veteran of the Wehrmacht. Had Herr Scherkenbach joined the Nazi party, or just signed the required allegiance to the Führer? How did that work back then? He didn't want to make Sherk uncomfortable or suspicious by badgering him with too many questions.

Early afternoon, Jack and Sherk left his parents' vacation house to visit the elder Scherkenbachs in Regensburg. Famous for its iconic medieval structures, the city rests at the confluence of the Danube, Naab, and Regen rivers about sixty-seven miles northeast of Munich.

Sherk drove north on the Autobahn in his dad's white Audi, Jack beside him gazing out the window at rolling hills, patches of woods, clean, tidy farms bathed in sunlight. Jack thought more about the grandfather.

As if reading his mind, Sherk said, "I just want to remind you not to question anything about my grandparents' war years, even though I'd have to translate."

"Gimme a little credit. I get the war's a touchy subject with you Germans." Jack glanced at the dashboard. "You're really barreling along, Sherk. How fast are you going?"

"Close to a hundred thirty kilometers. That's eighty miles an hour. Smooth road, right?" Just then a Mercedes whizzed by, leaving them in the dust.

"Good God, that guy must be doing over ninety. What's the speed limit?"

Sherk chuckled. "This is the Autobahn, Jack. No limit out here."

"I'll be damned. Maybe I'll move here. Get me a new Beemer." He paused. "Second thought, I'm too old to learn German." He continued taking in the scenery.

"Nice of your folks to let me stay with them." Jack preferred a hotel, but Sherk wouldn't agree. Every summer his parents rented the large house, which, as Sherk had promised, provided ample guest rooms for visitors. A lush backyard garden boasted comfortable patio furniture for socializing and meals, not to mention beer.

"They'd be insulted if you'd even tried to book a hotel. Mum loves feeding and fussing over guests."

"No kiddin' — been stuffed since we got here."

Sherk laughed. "Wait till you meet Oma this afternoon. At least we're only going for coffee." They planned to join Sherk's sister, Susi, who was staying with their parents until late June.

"Yeah, I remember what 'just coffee' means. Three kinds of sweets to go with it. My Irish relatives, same thing, but at least they speak English."

"Don't worry, Jack. Plenty of people to translate, but you'll hear mostly German since that's all Oma and Opa speak."

Sherk was ten when his parents immigrated to Chicago in the late seventies and settled in Lakeview on the north side. Since he and his sister had been immersed in English at a young age, they spoke with no accent.

As they approached Regensburg, Jack turned toward what Sherk identified as "the landmark thirteenth century Dom St. Peter Cathedral."

"Whoa, Sherk. We back in the Middle Ages?" The church's brown stone facade with twin Gothic steeples dominated the skyline. Its ornate pointed arches and stained-glass windows proved a mighty fortress indeed.

"Nothing looks rebuilt from the war. Was a lot of Regensburg bombed?"

"Not in city center," Sherk said. "Most ancient buildings here were safe. There were heavy Allied attacks around the outskirts, though."

"Very interesting. Maybe my old man came through here?" Jack had no idea.

"A good chance he did. Meanwhile, we're about to cross the Danube on this famous stone bridge. The French King, Louis the Seventh, used it to cross the river on his way to the Second Crusade."

"Yeah, it was built in the twelfth century." Jack allowed a playful tinge of smugness.

Sherk turned, looking at him as though he'd dropped from outer space. "How did you know that?"

"It was printed on the historical marker back there." Jack grunted. "Just blew my cover."

Sherk found a parking place a half block from the bridge. "No cars allowed, so we'll walk across. People can walk their bikes, but can't ride them over."

They emerged from the car and ambled across the Danube, taking in picturesque scenery of the river. Small cruise ships were docked at rocky banks, people of all ages wandered along snapping photographs.

After crossing the ancient bridge, they reached Old Town with tall sand-colored stone buildings, arched doorways, and narrow streets filled with strolling tourists. A distant street band played "Take the A Train". Not Ellington, but a decent enough sound.

Sherk pointed out an old theater with its ornate balcony and courtyard. A small boy scampered ahead of his mother who pushed a squalling baby in a stroller. Jack glanced away. At times the sight and squeals of children pierced him like a knife, prying open a twelve-year-old wound. Karen and Elizabeth; how he still missed them. He forced his thoughts back to the present.

After twenty minutes, they returned to the Audi sedan and Sherk soon wound his way through residential areas with homes side by side, nearly touching each other. Several minutes later, he stopped in front of a pale stone house with dark trim. The front yard was mostly garden space subdivided by raised wooden borders, including a covered greenhouse.

"Ma would go crazy seeing this yard," Jack looked around.

"Yeah, that's Liverwort and small shrubs surrounding white and red anemones. Full bloom this time of year."

"Anything beyond your expertise?"

"Very little, my man. Very little." He parked the car near the house, and they made their way up the sidewalk. Sherk's namesake, Karl Scherkenbach, stepped onto the porch, beaming at his guests. He welcomed Jack as if he were family. "Schön, dich zu sehen."

The silver-haired man could've been anyone's grandfather. Except most grandfathers hadn't fought against Stalin's army and lived to tell about it. But he would never tell. Dapper in a tan turtleneck and cardigan with suede elbow patches, he gazed at Jack with clear blue eyes, looking more like an aging philosophy professor than a veteran of the Wehrmacht.

Jack noticed his limp. He already knew the missing leg was forever interred beneath the Russian soil near a city once called Stalingrad.

His sacrifice for the Fatherland.

Jack shook the old gent's hand and stumbled over the greeting Sherk taught him. "Grüss Gott."

Herr Scherkenbach chuckled and carried on shaking Jack's hand, nodding and grinning.

Sherk's Oma Ella appeared and bustled everyone inside. Her hazel eyes sparkled behind small framed glasses, her smile like melted butter. She took Jack's arm, gesturing toward the ivory brocade sofa. "Hinsetzen, hinsetzen."

Chattering away in German, Oma Ella fussed over Jack, pointing toward coffee, stollen, and apple pastries tastefully arranged on a long dining table. An aroma of cinnamon floated through the air.

Sherk gave her a quick hug. "Oma, entspann dich." He turned to Jack. "I told her to relax."

Lost in a forest of guttural sounds, Jack smiled at her. "It's okay." He looked around at Sherk's family mingling in the living room. An attractive woman in her forties walked up to Jack and held out her hand.

"Hi, Jack. I'm Susi. It's nice to finally meet you." Her azure eyes twinkled.

Jack took her hand, warm in his. "Yes, Sherk's told me great things about you." Her skin looked like porcelain, flawlessly blending with her eyes and light reddish hair. Too bad she wasn't older and single. Sensing Sherk's disapproving glance, he decided he would stifle his thoughts. The guy was a mind-reader at times.

Soon everyone gathered around the table covered with embroidered white linen, rosebud china, gleaming silverware, linen napkins. A silver urn and fresh flower centerpiece completed the setting. All this for afternoon coffee?

After his grandparents were seated, Sherk pulled out a chair. "You can sit here, Jack."

The conversation flowed, with Oma Ella passing plates, and Sherk's mother, Greta, pouring coffee. Susi sat next to Jack. He handed her a serving of stollen that tasted like cardboard, but not everything can be wunderbar.

Jack tried to rinse the pastry down with coffee. "So this is how you and Sherk grew up?"

"Only when we visited Oma." She laughed and turned to him. "You actually do look like that movie actor. I'm sure you get sick of people telling you that."

Jack shrugged. "You get used to it." He seldom grew tired of the comparison; at least Neeson, fellow Irishman born the same year, was considered ruggedly handsome by some. Jack conveniently assumed this consideration also applied to him.

Jack's black hair, graduating to salty the past ten years, was still thick and shiny, his blue eyes darker than the Scherkenbachs' lighter hue.

Twenty minutes later sitting across from Sherk's grandfather, whose polished cane leaned on his armrest, Jack felt like he'd been teleported into 1940's Europe. Bookshelves of mahogany, Persian rugs, and a carved armoire displayed themselves with Old World ambience. The smell of coffee lingered in the air. Only thing missing were violinists playing Strauss waltzes.

Listening to German conversation amongst Sherk's relatives, Jack was a world away from Chicago. It struck him that these gracious, welcoming people were America's former enemy. What would his old man think? His son drinking coffee with a former soldier of the Third Reich. Or possibly a bona fide Nazi.

But then again, based on the letter, his father himself may have —

Jack checked his thoughts. Focus on here and now.

He glanced around at the jovial faces. How did this amiable family survive the war? They looked, dressed, acted like ordinary people. For the first time, Jack truly understood the wartime axiom of 'brother against brother'. Hell, his old man could've fought against Sherk's grandpa and great uncles.

Immersed in a world of foreign tongues and genteel surroundings, Jack's thoughts wandered back to the real reason he'd made this trip. He needed to tell Sherk about the letter.

Soon.

CHAPTER 3

The next morning Jack and Sherk sat in the backyard garden polishing off a hearty breakfast of scrambled eggs, Weisswurst, and toast with tart plum jam. Birds sang like an orchestra of flutes throughout vibrant green trees, the yard smelling of freshly cut grass.

Jack took a bite of meat. "Never eaten white sausage before, but gotta admit it's damn good."

"The best Bavaria has to offer," Sherk said. "They process it by —"

"Okay, I said I like the stuff. Don't push it." A pang of guilt struck him. *Don't be so short. Allow Sherk to strut his stuff. At least until I've told him about the letter.*

"Sorry, Sherk. Tell me about the process. I'm all ears."

Sherk spoke, but Jack paid no attention. Instead, he was lost in warm garden sunshine, with a lavender smell of flowers. Lily pads drifted atop a small pond with greenish water, a breeze whispered through willow and chestnut trees. A distant church bell chimed.

Perhaps sensing Jack's disinterest, Sherk wiped his mouth and put his napkin by his plate. "How about a visit to BMW headquarters? Then we'll hit the Hofbräuhaus —"

Jack started to rise, but hesitated. "Hold on, Sherk." He sat back, gazing into his friend's eyes. "There's something I want to show you. Something I've been putting off."

Jack fished a small envelope from his pocket and glanced toward the back door. "Will we be alone for a while?"

Sherk raised his eyebrows. "Sure. My folks should be gone until noon."

"Before you read this, I need to explain." Jack eased the letter from its envelope, cleared his throat. "A few months ago, Ma uncovered an old box of my pa's, full of stuff he'd saved from the war. She wanted us kids to go through it, see if anything interested us. Tommy had looked already, so I took the box just to humor her. Figured I didn't need any of my old man's crap."

Jack placed the letter on the table. He explained that he'd found it stuck inside a booklet, and almost missed it. "It was written mainly in German, so I got online and googled the translation. The woman used some English, probably so Pa could understand. Damn near fell off my chair when I read it." He handed Sherk the letter.

After reading the single page, Sherk pushed a blond strand from his forehead. "Gott im Himmel, what did you do?"

"I called Tommy. He'd seen it and put it back. We couldn't accept our old man had a fling with a Fräulein during the war. Doesn't add up. If you'd been around him—" He let his voice trail off.

"At first, we were gonna let it go. Keep the letter. Not tell Ma. We're still not certain she's in the dark about it. But why would she purposely hide it in a box instead of destroying it? Doesn't make sense." Jack shook his head.

"Right," Sherk agreed. "There's enough English in it for her to get the gist of the message. It's quite intense, about how true love is so painful. Especially at the end when—" Sherk scanned the letter. "Fräulein Schröder writes both she and your dad, John, were damaged, and she always would be." He handed the letter back to Jack. "She sounds like a decent sort though, wishing him happiness. Für immer und ewig."

Sherk thought for a minute and pushed back his chair. "More coffee?"

"Yeah. Got anything to add to it?"

He apparently read Jack's mind. "Sure, I'll bring some good brandy for you. Asbach, truly top drawer. Not whisky, but better than Jameson."

"Fat chance of that, but it'll do."

Jack and Sherk had been partners in Bridgeport PD, a division of the vast Chicago department. After years of wrestling PTSD-causing demons from his past, along with frustrations on the job, Jack had never regretted stomping off in a rage a couple months ago. He remained friends with Sherk, whose wife, undergoing ovarian cancer treatment, could not make their annual trip to Munich in June. She had convinced him to go without her, to invite Jack in her stead. After all, she was between treatments, doing fine, and her parents were with her to help care for the kids.

Tommy had urged Jack to pursue the letter's origin. "Look at it as a missing persons case, Jack. Track down this Ariana Schröder. She's most likely dead by now, but give it a shot."

"You're right. I gotta try."

Jack realized his brother's need to understand sank deeper than the surface. As the oldest son, Tommy bore the brunt of his old man's drunken rages, at times standing in harm's way like a sentry protecting his younger brothers.

"He's always in my head," Tommy had said over beers one night. "Never been able to forgive the bastard. Possibly the key to his fury is this woman. Something might have happened with her, may explain his outrage. Hell, I'm no shrink, but I wanna find out if we can."

At the time, Jack was hesitant. Should they dig up the past? Could the search backfire in some strange way?

●　　　●　　　●　　　●　　　●

Sherk returned with more coffee and a bottle of Asbach. Jack splashed a liberal amount into his cup, took a gulp. "Ahhh. Gotta admit, not bad." He wouldn't tell Sherk the stuff didn't hold a candle to Jameson. Brandy or whisky? No comparison.

"So, you want to try and get information on Ariana Schröder?"

"Yeah. Think you can spare some time to help? My German's a little rusty"

Sherk hesitated. His eyes looked to his right, then to the floor. "Yeah, I suppose."

Jack's guess was Sherk felt slighted. Offended that he'd waited to spring the letter on him. "Sorry. I should've told you before. I just thought — and Tommy — " He told himself to shut up.

Sherk's lips were tightly pressed. He crossed his arms. "So that's really why you came on the trip? To locate this woman?"

Jack couldn't tell if Sherk was pissed or just annoyed. "I can't lie to you, man. Yeah, it was the main reason, but hey, I'm liking Munich and your relatives — "

"Save it, Jack." He cleared his throat. "It's okay. I'm a little on edge. I'm more worried about Erica than I want to admit to you and the family."

Jack was relieved to find that out. Naturally, Sherk would be stressed about his wife. He took a drink of coffee. "No need to explain. We can let it go for now."

Sherk swiped at an insect on the table. They sat without speaking.

•   •   •   •   •

Sherk finished his last bite of sausage. "I wish you would've told me sooner about the letter. I think you duped me, Jack, but—"

"No, wait, I didn't mean—"

"Let's not talk any more about it." Sherk put his fork down. "I'm ready to help you out."

"Okay, thanks." He hadn't seen his friend react like that before. Guess he should quit taking his good nature for granted.

Jack finished his toast in silence. Before the trip, his mother instructed him to visit Dachau to see the site where John Bailey's Infantry Division liberated the first Nazi concentration camp.

You have to go, Jacky. You may be the only one in the family to ever see where your father ended up in the war. It would be a tribute to him to visit the place.

He scoffed at the memory. His mother probably knew more than she admitted. Always covered up her husband's drinking and bursts of violence, claiming it was the war that made him that way. Never his fault.

Maybe he'd visit Dachau. Maybe not. Right now, he'd focus on the letter.

Sherk was a good sport for helping in his search, although guilt persisted to nudge the edges of his mind. Jack poured himself more coffee and doctored it with a healthy splash of Asbach. He willed himself to relax and appreciate his friend's good nature. "Let's get to it. Where do we start?"

Chapter 4

Sherk seemed to perk up. He paused and drained his coffee. "The first thing we do is a public record search. Let's go inside to use my laptop. Easier to see than the phone."

The men cleared the table and carried their dishes to the kitchen. Sherk loaded the dishwasher while Jack poured himself coffee.

In the adjoining dining room, they settled at the table and Sherk powered up his laptop. The room was airy, spacious with the same neutral colors as the rest of the house. Everything tan, beige, white. Modern décor and leather furniture juxtaposed with the sedate, traditional furnishings of the elder Scherkenbachs' home in Regensburg.

Jack looked on as Sherk hunkered over the monitor, clicking, searching.

"She doesn't show up in the quick search. Too many Schröders to investigate. Let me detail it a little." Sherk proceeded mumbling to himself, figuring aloud.

Growing impatient, Jack stood. "Gonna get a sweet roll. Want anything?"

Sherk declined, so Jack left to retrieve a pastry from a platter on the counter. He selected a strawberry tart, but passed on the stollen. That stuff was drier than a ten-year-old fruitcake used as a doorstop.

He sat in the kitchen and ate. Didn't want to get crumbs on the dining room table's linen placemats.

When he returned, Sherk didn't look up. "We may end up going to Einwohnermeldeampt and see—"

"Hold on, man. What in hell—"

"Sorry, Jack. Keep forgetting. It's the resident registration office. Every German citizen living legally in the country has to register at an address. I did their high-speed search, but it doesn't indicate if she married, has another name, where her last—"

"Yeah, I get the picture. I figured it was a long shot."

"Giving up already?" Sherk shook his head. "Come on, Jack, we have not yet begun to fight."

"A relief, man. Not your usual Shakespeare. Not Patrick Henry. An American general, right?"

"John Paul Jones, captain of—"

"Yeah, yeah. I remember. Not in the mood for a history lesson." Damned if he could recall the circumstances of Jones, but he wasn't about to admit it.

"Give me a few more minutes while I try other leads."

Five minutes later, Sherk looked up. "That's all I can turn up online. Let's head for the Einwohner—sorry, the registration office. Not sure if they'll give us details, but if we don't luck out there, we'll contact the German Red Cross Tracing Service. It's been around since the Franco-German war back in—"

"Look, I hate to be a prick, but can't hack a lecture right now." Jack hoped he wouldn't regret requesting Sherk's help, but he'd be lost with the language barrier. Guess he'd have to put up with the dissertations. Contrary to popular opinion, Jack soon realized many Germans don't speak English. Particularly older folks. But no problem if you're on a tour where the guides take you to popular tourist, English-friendly sites.

Sherk studied the monitor. "Okay, the Red Cross traces displaced and missing persons from wartime, and it's grown a lot since the second world war, as you can imagine. There's an office here in Munich, so that's a good start."

Jack's heart thumped. Perhaps they'd luck out in the end. He wasn't sure he wanted to find the woman, but too late now. He'd promised Tommy. What happened to his own determination?

Sherk clicked on a map. "The Red Cross isn't far from the registration office. Shouldn't take more than half an hour to hit both places." He looked up. "For our Ariana Schröder request, we need to state a reason for the search, like wanting to reconnect with a family member."

Jack thought a minute. "You mean we can't just put in a name?"

"Doesn't work like that." Sherk read the screen. "You need grounds for an investigation. Finding a family member is first, but there are other vague goals, like we're hunting for a government official for something.

It gets too complicated." He shook his head and stood. "Even so, let's go for it."

"Guess we dream up our own motive then." Jack rose from the table and followed Sherk through the living room.

"Right." Sherk turned, furrowing his brow. "Why would you need to contact Ariana?"

"Damned if I know," Jack said. "I guess curiosity about my old man's wartime fling won't cut it?"

"Highly doubtful. We'll rack our brains harder."

Ten minutes later, Sherk pulled the Audi out of the narrow driveway. They drove past a canal of the Isar River that flows through Munich. Bright green trees lined boulevards.

"Nice area. How did your parents find their house?"

Sherk slowed down for a bus ahead. "The area is called Bogenhausen, and we grew up a few miles away. So they were familiar with the area, and could find their way around. They can walk to restaurants plus a fitness center nearby. Easy access to transportation so Dad doesn't have to drive all over."

"Your folks ever consider moving back here permanently?"

"Sometimes. They'd like to be near our grandparents and cousins, but they've got a good community in Chicago."

Jack gazed at a row of bungalows, their window boxes overflowing with red and orange flowers. The Windy City couldn't hold a candle to this charming European enclave. He almost said this aloud, but bit his tongue. "Yeah, probably hard to figure what's best."

The traffic thinned as they headed down Oberföhringer Strasse and picked up 2R south.

They passed tan concrete buildings, a mixture of high rises, apartments, condos, businesses. Oak and chestnut trees lined boulevards, men and women of all ages strolled or hurried along the sidewalks. Jack stared out the window. "Can't get over how clean everything looks. No slums in Munich?"

Sherk stopped at a light. "Sure, there are some seedy areas, but they're easy to avoid."

"The Germans look a lot thinner than Americans. Must be all that walking. Never seen so many skinny broads wearing black."

"Haven't you heard?" Sherk chuckled. "Black is the new black. Mum tells Susi she should wear more red, but my sis says she saves the bright colors for Chicago." Sherk slowed down as the road narrowed into two lanes. "Looks like construction ahead. Should've checked traffic reports."

As vehicles slowed to a standstill, drivers honked, stretching their heads out car windows to check the holdup. "Crap. Don't need this," Jack muttered.

"Shouldn't be too long, but usually it's not this bad," Sherk said with his usual annoying upbeat attitude.

Fifteen minutes and fifty yards later, Jack's patience reached a boiling point.

"Scheisse, man, isn't there any other way to go?" Jack had learned the German vulgarity from Sherk's father, who thankfully wasn't as morally upright as his son.

"Yeah, I'm contemplating changing plans. We'll skip the Registration office for now and get out of this mess. Cross the river to Maximilianstrasse. The Red Cross office is in that area."

"Yeah, anything's better than sitting here all day."

They crawled along for several minutes, then turned right onto Prinzregentenstrasse, where traffic was lighter. Sedans replaced vans and trucks; drivers drove at a slower pace. "We're heading west toward the river again, backtracking, but at least it's a scenic route." Sherk eased behind a parked car by the curb of a shady park. He turned off the engine and pointed out Jack's window.

"There's a monument of Richard Wagner. You'd recognize der Ring des—sorry, his Ring cycle opera, if nothing else—"

"Don't take this the wrong way, but—"

"The music from the four Ring operas, *Die Walküre*, "Ride of the Valkyries" famous as the theme from—"

"May come as a shock," Jack said, "but I know the thing. Happened to see the rerun of *Apocalypse Now* a few months ago. So there, Professor."

The granite statue of Wagner reclined on a huge circular armchair, one hand grasping the end of a musical score. Tall, morose trees surrounded the statue, giving an illusion of Wagner contemplating his next opera while sitting in the Black Forest.

"Gotta admit, this is amazing," Jack said. "Here we are a few yards from a busy street and this guy's sittin' here like the King of Bavaria. I suppose it's been here for ages?"

"Actually, it was built in 1913, so not as old as you may imagine. Wagner was born in Leipzig around 1813, and the monument was commissioned by Ludwig III as a memorial—"

"Gotcha. Should've learned by now not to bother with a simple question."

"Yeah, Erica learned that a long time ago." Sherk pushed the Audi's start button. "Ready to go?"

Sherk's wife must weigh heavily on his mind, certainly weightier than locating Jack's father's German romance.

"Yeah, by the way, how is Erica?" The last Sherk said, her test results were getting better because of chemo treatments.

"She texted last night that she feels good. More scans are coming up next week."

Jack couldn't come up with anything profound to say, but at least he'd said something. He kept silent as they drove.

•　　　•　　　•　　　•　　　•

Five minutes later, they reached Maximilianpark, a quiet, tree-lined area beside the Isar River bordered by walking and jogging trails, along with sled hills popular in winter.

"Another forest." Jack lowered his window and stuck his head out.

"Yes, now you can brace yourself for another cultural treat."

"As long as we don't have to get our asses out of the car. Just so much a guy like me can take."

"There it is." Sherk slowed down as they approached a sparkling, aqua pool with a dolphin-shaped fountain spewing water toward the sky.

Easing along left of the round-about, they neared the historic gilded Angel of Peace monument glittering in the sun high above deep green trees.

"Hey, that looks familiar," Jack said. "In one sentence or less, what is it?"

"The Angel of Peace was erected in 1899 as a reminder of twenty-five peaceful years following the Franco-German War, and you notice the small temple underneath—"

"I said one sentence, man."

Sherk laughed. "Sentence wasn't done yet, Jack." He gazed admiringly at the monument. "No worries. We'll come back another day and go inside to see portraits of emperors and Bavarian rulers, not to mention gold mosaics."

"Yeah, gotta do that." Jack had other things on his mind at the moment. He'd never been interested in art, but years ago Karen had introduced him to Monet and Van Gogh, whom he now mildly appreciated.

Heading around the monument plaza, they crossed the river and made their way toward the Red Cross center. Sherk turned south where the area became more commercialized with high rises and modern buildings. He merged onto a freeway, and twenty minutes later they reached a gray, modern multi-storied building set apart on a tree-lined knoll.

"Here we are." Sherk pulled into a parking lot in front.

"This is the Red Cross building?" Jack was surprised the place looked so new.

"Yes, there are several sites, but the main Bavarian office is in this building."

"Guess I was expecting something out of wartime Munich, like the Rathaus."

"Sorry to disappoint you, Jack. Just another concrete and glass building you'd see in Chicago."

They stepped out of the car and walked up a dozen front steps.

"Here goes nothing," Jack said. A knot formed in his gut as he followed Sherk through the revolving door. Did he truly want to find Ariana Schröder? What would he do if he did?

"Not getting cold feet, are you, Jack? We can turn back if you want."

"No. Let's do this. Get it over with," Jack muttered as he tried to ignore increasing dampness crawling under his armpits. What had he gotten himself into?

CHAPTER 5

Several hours later, Sherk drove to a pub called the Ludwig Keller a couple blocks off 2R on the way home. "I understand you're chomping at the bit to get more details on the search, but how 'bout a late lunch? This place is quiet. We can talk in peace."

"Fine by me. Always up for a drink, in case you hadn't noticed."

They parked down the block from a brown, unadorned stone building. "Looks like a hole in the wall, but I trust ya." Actually, it was Jack's kind of place.

Dark and spartan, the room was occupied by one other customer sitting at the bar. Two large gilded-framed pictures of Bavarian kings hung proudly on dark paneled walls near the entryway. Traditional beer steins with ornamental pewter lids sat on each table. Sherk led the way to a spot in a small alcove across the room. "Should be quiet enough for you, Jack. I'm barely aware of any music."

A middle-aged woman of hefty girth waddled over with menus in hand. Sherk ordered a Pilsner for Jack, a Riesling for himself.

She returned in five minutes with their drinks. "Wass kann ich dich zum essen bringen?"

"How does the bratwurst sampler sound?" Sherk looked up from his menu.

"I'll go for it." Jack rubbed the frosty glass, admiring the amber hue of good strong beer.

They discussed more details Sherk had learned at the Red Cross office; it would probably take a couple more days to discover something concrete after meeting with certain officials and clerks. "I'll just wait till I'm done with the process to tell you everything. I used my powers of persuasion, so therefore, we just may luck out."

Jack restrained himself from griping it was a matter of hurry up and wait, but he'd hoped they'd soon dig up something about Ariana. He had no right to complain, though. He'd never get anywhere on his own.

After ten minutes, Jack's glass was nearing empty, so he headed for the bar and ordered another. Back at the table, he said, "I like this place. Doesn't look too great from the outside, but who cares." He wiped moisture from the side of his glass with a napkin and drank.

"I just got a text from Erica. She's tired, but otherwise, she's fine. She has tests in another week or so. I can't help having second thoughts about leaving her halfway across the world to—" He glanced sideways.

"Sorry, man," Jack said. "But her folks are there, and with all the medical advances these days, I'm sure she'll be fine." Well aware his words were just platitudes, they were the best he could do.

Sherk nodded. "We're hoping." He looked at Jack. "Maybe it's the wine, but I'm gonna ask you something. You can tell me it's none of my business."

Jack sensed what was coming. "Go ahead."

Sherk cleared his throat. "Well, we've known each other about two or three years, and worked as partners. Spent a lot of time together. I'm generally aware of what happened in Ireland with your family, and it's a painful subject, but I'd like to know what actually took place." He waited. "That is, if you're comfortable taking about it."

Jack sighed. "You're right. I don't talk about it, except to my shrinks and Tommy. They tell me I should talk more, though. It's a way to keep Karen and Elizabeth honored, that their lives were worthy, and not to pretend they never existed."

"I'll tell you, Jack, that's the wisest thing that ever came out of your mouth." Sherk grinned.

"Can't take credit. I'm quoting my shrink who finally eased me off the PTSD nightmares and stress."

"So, you were on a trip to Ireland when—"

"Our dinner's coming," Jack said, glancing at the waitress approaching their table.

"Hier sind Sie ja," she said, placing two plates of steaming meat surrounded by golden potato salad, creamy cole slaw, and sauerkraut on the table.

"Sure smells good." Jack breathed in spicy aromas of smoked bratwurst. He spread brown mustard on the sausage and took a bite. "Delicious."

They ate in silence for a few moments. Jack put his fork down. "Okay, now's as good a time as any to start. Yeah, we were in Ireland for our eighth anniversary. The trip was a gift from Karen's folks, and we took Elizabeth, who was almost five. We were in and around Belfast visiting relatives. We'd been aware of news about a bombing south of there a couple weeks before, but never thought much about it. Like being told about disasters in other places. You never dream it'll happen to you."

He paused and took a swig of beer. "Christ, I'll never fall into that trap again."

Sherk shook his head. "True, people are convinced they're immune to distant catastrophes."

Jack finished his sausage and coleslaw. "One day we drove to Omagh, this little town where my uncle lives, almost two hours west of Belfast. Scenery like you see in a brochure. Perfect day, sunny, mild." He cleared his throat. "It was August, the beginning of the school year, so a lot of people were shopping for their kids. There was a carnival in the town center, so we walked around for a while, Elizabeth wanting to play all the games like tossing little sandbags into holes, stuff like that. She ended up winning a big purple bracelet." The memory prompted a bittersweet grimace. His throat tightened.

"Take your time," Sherk said.

Jack took a deep breath. "Then we found a pub that served food and ice cream. I was at the bar ordering beer for me and Karen, a cone for Elizabeth. The bartender was talking to some guys, telling them he'd just got word of a bomb threat at the courthouse, and they were evacuating people. I wondered if we should get the hell out, and the guy told me the building was a good distance from where we were, so he wasn't worried. They get their share of threats."

"Oh God," Sherk said quietly.

Jack looked over as the front door opened and several more customers arrived, choosing a table across the room. He looked out the window at a large black dog plodding beside an elderly woman in a plain faded dress.

"I told Karen about the threat, so we practically gulped our beer and decided to head home." Jack wiped his mouth with a paper napkin. "But I needed the men's room, so Karen said they'd wait outside on the sidewalk for me. Who would've guessed that my decision to use the john would be a life or death choice?"

Sherk nodded, fully aware what was coming.

Jack clenched his jaw. "Yeah, just finished washing my hands, opened the door, and that's when it happened. A huge crash, like the earth opened up. It didn't register what the hell it was. An earthquake? It was like I was suspended in mid-air, looking down on myself." He wiped his brow. "Then I was in all this rubble, couldn't walk, my legs wouldn't work. I must've lost memory. Bottom line, I eventually made it outside, calling for Karen, Elizabeth. People covered in blood, the smell of something like burning rubber, and oddly enough, I later realized I'd tasted metal."

"Sounds like a war zone," Sherk said.

"That's how people described it afterwards. Debris, shattered glass, bodies." Jack looked out the window again. "I can't remember everything, but my gut told me they were both dead. I saw Elizabeth's—" He coughed. "Her arm was on a slab of concrete. Just—just her arm. But it was hers. She'd won the purple bracelet at the fair."

Sherk turned pale, visibly shaken. He placed his hand on Jack's arm. "Good Christ, Jack. You don't need to say anymore."

"It's okay. Done it before." He paused. "A good Samaritan type guy wondered who I was looking for, helped me. People all over the place, calling out for family and friends. He and I found Elizabeth and then Karen, lying face down. I turned her over, and I thought she was alive. She fluttered her eyes, and then looked right at me. I shook her, yelled, but in a second, she was gone. I tell myself I was the last thing she saw, but—"

"That's a good thought to hang on to." Sherk took a drink. "This happened when? Twelve years ago?"

"Almost. Twelve years this August." Jack's eye twitched. "Seems like a century ago."

Sherk didn't speak for several seconds. "Thanks for telling me. I can see how it's taken you years to come to terms with it."

Jack scoffed. "Yeah, shrinks and other experts talk about a 'new normal.' Let me tell ya something. There ain't no new normal, or any kind of frickin' normal."

They sat in silence. Jack drained his beer. "I was a mess for months, hell, years. Tommy was the biggest help. I got hammered one night, called him, said it was all over. Had my gun ready."

Sherk waited.

"He made me promise not to do anything till he came over. He damn near banged the door down before I got up and let him in. He managed to talk me out of it."

Sherk said, "He's a good man, your brother. And after your ordeal, I can see why people don't want to talk about the war, losing people. Way too painful."

"Yeah." Jack looked around. "Tell ya, right now I'm beat, had enough. I'm ready for some fresh air."

Sherk caught the waitress's eye, and she came with their check.

"This is on me, Jack."

"Thanks, pal. I'll take it."

Jack inhaled the mild, refreshing air as they walked out of the pub.

"Ready for a nap?" Sherk turned toward the car.

"You bet." Jack was drained. He hadn't purged like that since his last shrink appointment. After unloading his past on Sherk, the possibility of meeting his father's wartime Fräulein would be a piece of cake. It was still a long shot, but what else did he have to do?

One thing was for sure; he was exhausted. Might skip his Ambien tonight.

CHAPTER 6
Munich, three days later

Jack awoke to rain tapping on the roof as dawn crept through the window blinds. Perhaps the rain was an omen of coming events. He could still bail out of the trip he and Sherk planned for today.

After stumbling from the bed, he snuck into the bathroom across the hall. Didn't want to wake Sherk. He splashed cold water on his face, returned to his room, and crawled under the covers. He tried to sleep, but the call to his brother last night picked at his brain when he had updated him on the search for Ariana Schröder.

"You'll be shocked at this," Jack had said, "In a couple days' time, we found out she's still alive, and we found her address. That is, Sherk did. He jumped through all kinds of hoops, but he managed to locate her home."

Jack told his brother about the Red Cross center, how Sherk conversed with two officials, who bent a rule or two, helping to locate Frau Schröder under the guise of a possible relative in the States trying to locate her.

"I didn't understand all of Sherk's negotiations and arm-twisting, but he made it look easier than I ever thought, mainly since we figured she'd have a married name. Bottom line she's widowed, last name is Gunther. She's eighty-seven now, lives in a nursing home in Weimar."

Tommy sucked in his breath. "God, Jack. Never thought you'd do it. Let's see, Pa would be what now? Ninety-two, so she's younger. About the same age as Ma."

Jack felt like the lead actor in a Lifetime movie. Wartime romance, forbidden love, buried secrets. He had explained to Tommy that the woman's family had lived in the village of Dachau for years, and some relatives remained to this day. His brother hadn't realized Dachau was a town as well as the name of the infamous concentration camp, the source of their father's nightmares.

●   ●   ●   ●   ●

Now as dawn was breaking and rain splattering the windows, Jack grew uneasy about their plans to drive to Weimar today, stay the night, and visit the assisted living place where Ariana Schröder Gunther resided. What would he say to the woman? Would she kick him out of the room?

After breakfast Jack and Sherk took off for Weimar, a small city about 245 miles north of Munich. Jack was familiar with the term, Weimar Republic, but didn't recall details. Knowing Sherk would have hours to enlighten him with a tutorial, he hadn't bothered googling the place.

Damn downpour turned into a deluge. Jack hated rain. Always intensified the gloom of his life, never mind the messiness. Back home, Boone, his aging dog of blended ancestry, would track in mud on floors and furniture. No wonder Ma refused to dog sit for Jack with her new beige sofa.

They drove north on the A9, the easiest route to Weimar, passing an exit to Ingolstadt, rain relentless, pelting trees and buildings. Bending forward, Sherk squinted at blurred shadows through the windshield, wipers clacking back and forth in a frenzy. Traffic slowed down to fifty miles per hour, plenty fast for Jack.

"We gonna have to stop?" he said. "Can't see for shit. I mean scheisse."

"You're starting to grasp the German language, at least the important parts." Sherk grinned as he inched around a semi. "No, we don't need to stop. I can still see the white line."

"Can't remember rain this bad. Pain in the ass."

"It should let up soon." Sherk, eternal optimist. Perhaps he'd be right this time.

"I'm gonna kick myself for opening my big mouth, but what's the history of Weimar?"

"Fascinating, Jack. Goethe and Schiller spent much time there, along with artists like Klee, Kandinsky, and Liszt, the composer, just to name a few. The Weimar Republic was established after World War I and lasted fourteen years, ending in 1933, when Hitler took over."

Sherk switched lanes to pass and escape the spray of another truck, visibility still poor, but tolerable. "Remember last week when we drank beer and walked around Odeonsplatz near the old Rathaus? I pointed out the monument with pillars and lions in front. That's the Field Marshall's Hall, and — "

"Oh yeah. The Beer Hall Putsch happened there. A bunch of Nazis were shot and killed and Hitler was arrested, then sent to prison. That's where he wrote *Mein Kampf*." Jack's interest piqued in spite of himself.

"Proud of you, Jack. You're smarter than you look."

"Always the comedian. So, the Weimar bit lasted how long after the putsch? Ten years?"

"Right again, pal. When Hindenburg appointed Hitler as chancellor, the Nazi party gained control."

"And the rest, is, how shall I put it delicately, bullshit."

Sherk turned the wipers down a notch. "True. Munich has the regrettable distinction of being the birthplace of National Socialism."

"In other words, Nazism. But why Munich? You'd figure it would've started in Berlin."

Sherk shook his head. "Hitler found it fairly easy to get followers because of Munich's circles of right-wing and anti-Semitic ideologies. The Munich Agreement of 1938 pretty much launched the war."

"Oh, yeah, that's when Chamberlain flew back and told the Brits he'd stopped another war?" Jack was proud of himself for remembering that detail.

"Right. Prime Minister Neville Chamberlain was truly naïve. Hitler pulled the wool over his eyes, but Churchill saw right through Hitler." Sherk adjusted his glasses. "Isn't this fascinating stuff, Jack?"

"Never thought I'd see the day I'd agree with ya, but yeah, gotta admit it ain't bad."

The rain turned into a lackluster patter, and dark clouds no longer hid welcome sunlight.

Jack stared out the window at clumps of fir trees along with occasional auto factories, the cleanest countryside he'd seen, except in Ireland twelve years ago. He willed himself not to brood about the deaths of Karen and Elizabeth. The struggle was constant. The day they were killed by that IRA car bombing in the center of that small town near Belfast would be forever etched on his brain.

Driving full speed again, Sherk said, "Okay. Now we're rolling. Should get to Weimer in a couple hours. Getting hungry yet?"

"Nah. Let's just drive." Jack was ready to relax and close his eyes. Absorbing Sherk's history lesson taxed his brain, but thoughts of Ariana elbowed their way into his mind. Was he doing the right thing by dredging up the past?

He told himself to just relax, quit ruminating. What's the worst that could happen?

CHAPTER 7
Weimar

The dashboard clock showed twelve-thirty when Sherk turned onto the A4 toward Weimar.

"Almost there, Jack. It's too early to check into the hotel, so how about lunch before we track down Ariana Schröder Gunther?" During the final part of his search, Sherk had discovered Ariana's husband, Walter, died many years ago. They had one daughter.

Jack's stomach grumbled. "Yeah, lets find a pub. I'm in the mood for some bratwurst and beer."

Sherk agreed, so twenty minutes later, he turned north onto 85 and made his way into the city. The rain quit at last, and the sun teased, peeking around gray clouds.

"Another clean, green German town," Jack said as he took in tidy houses and apartment buildings. Some homes were mansions, sprawling over lush, landscaped lawns. "Must rent rooms out in those places."

"Some, but not all. Lots of old money around here." Sherk veered off the road onto Berkaer Strasse, where pavements narrowed and neighborhoods became dense with trees.

"Looks like Lincoln Park," Jack said. People, young and old alike, sauntered or jogged along winding paths. "Where's our hotel?"

"It's behind us a few blocks." Sherk turned a corner. "We'll eat lunch at the best place in town. Right in the center of Weimar across from the Stadtschloss. Another captivating story, Jack. The restaurant is Weimar's oldest coffeehouse, and—"

"Hold on, man. Coffeehouse? I don't need Starbucks. I need a real place that serves booze."

Sherk scoffed. "Don't worry. They have a great list of German brews, as well as a reputable wine offering."

They drove around narrow streets, twisting and turning amongst ancient faded stone buildings. Young mothers pushed strollers along cobblestone sidewalks while bikers pedaled past with seeming purpose.

"Now that the sun's out, we can sit on the terrace," Sherk said.

They reached a bustling open market area filled with booths displaying flowers, crafts, grilled meats, and baked goods. Jack hoped Sherk wouldn't suggest browsing the place. It reminded him of Karen, who had loved shopping. Their last day together in Ireland before—he forced his thoughts into the here and now.

Sherk parked along a shady street a couple blocks from the market place, and they made their way on cobbled sidewalks toward the restaurant.

As they turned onto Gruner Markt, Sherk pointed. "There it is. Residenze Café, built in the 1830's, if memory serves."

"Too fancy for me," Jack grumbled.

"No worries. It's more casual inside."

A modern light gray façade overlooked an open terrace with large green striped umbrellas shading cloth-covered tables. The patio spilled over with diners eating and drinking. Waiters hustled about. Sherk pointed to a menu posted at the door.

"There's everything from cream of asparagus with wild garlic pesto to Thuringian bratwurst."

"Like I said, too fancy. Just gimme a beer and burger."

Sherk shrugged off Jack's comment and strode into the main room. A young waitress indicated they could sit anywhere. Sherk pointed to a booth alongside the front windows. "We're lucky to find a space. It's always crowded in summer."

As they sat down, Jack said, "Smells good. Must be the sausage." He eyed the shiny wood bar across the room. As if on cue, a pudgy middle-aged waiter appeared.

"Guten Tag." He placed menus on the table and offered drink orders.

Sherk studied the wine list. "I'd recommend Schwarzbier, Jack. It's a regional dark beer. Could be similar to Guinness. Sound good?"

"Right now I'll take anything."

"Okay, and I'm going to opt for red wine." He looked at the waiter. "Ein Nordheimer Vögelein und Krombacher Dark, bitte."

"Bitte schön." The waiter plodded off.

After Sherk pointed out various elaborate dinners on the menu, Jack settled on Thuringian Bratwurst with hearty sauerkraut and fried potatoes.

"I'll regret this, but what does 'thur—whatever mean?"

"Weimar is in the Federal State of Thuringia. Similar to our counties in the States."

"You managed to answer a question in one sentence, Professor. Not bad."

•   •   •   •   •

An hour later, stuffed with food and drink, the men left the restaurant and emerged into now-brilliant sunshine. People either meandered or scurried about; everything seemed to burst with yellows, reds, blues. Sherk pointed out the massive stone Stadtschloss and its adjoining museum across the street. "The old Gestapo headquarters were in the former royal stables off the courtyard."

"That's a kicker—former Gestapo place right amidst fancy shops, normal people walking around. Plus, look at the sun shining on the windows making it look like something out of a picture book. Seems bizarre."

"It's a real juxtaposition, all right," Sherk agreed.

"Smart ass."

Walking along, Jack realized he didn't feel as far removed from the war since coming to Germany. It was closer, more personal than the distant battles he'd slept through during high school history class. He'd bet the old geezers milling about town would have plenty of grim stories to tell. But no doubt those words would remain locked in their vaults.

When they reached the car, Jack said, "I dunno, man. Having second thoughts. Nosing into someone's past like we're about to. What if Ariana doesn't want to reveal anything?"

"We'll find out soon enough. Be positive."

"I am. I'm positive this ain't gonna work out."

"Well, then why are we here?" Sherk's irritation palpable.

"Aw, chill out. It's just me," Jack scoffed. "After all these years, you know I'm full of hot air. And horseshit."

Sherk ignored him, started the car, and made his way on a winding paved street that stopped at a crossroad. "If we turned north here, we'd head toward Buchenwald, about fifteen minutes away." One thing about Sherk. He didn't stay pissed for long.

"No shit. I didn't know that was around here. Was it bigger than Dachau?"

"Yeah. One of the earliest camps built in Germany during the mid-thirties. Would you be interested in seeing it tomorrow?"

"Nah. Gonna see Dachau. That'll be enough."

"Right." Sherk adjusted the visor. "Well, are you ready to meet Frau Schröder, or Gunther more precisely?"

"I guess. Can't put it off much longer." Aware of the heaviness in his gut, Jack regretted devouring every bite of sauerkraut and potatoes.

"If this works out, Jack, and we actually meet the woman, you need to decide what you want me to tell her. I'm sure she doesn't speak English."

Jack gazed out the window at tree-lined curbs and stately homes. "Can't decide what to say." Why was his chest hammering? As if he didn't know.

"Let's just see if she can have visitors," Sherk said. "She may be bed-ridden, who can tell?"

"Yeah, we'll wing it."

They drove north and passed the picturesque Weimar Atrium. Sherk slowed down. "Almost there."

Jack wiped his brow, took a deep breath. "Oh, God. Actually, this whole secret letter thing is more of a woman's deal. What do I know about talking to little old ladies, except when they were witnesses back in my cop days?"

"Don't chicken out now. We've come this far."

The neighborhood was thick with trees and shrub-like fences surrounding pockets of open land. Sherk stopped the car and turned right onto a brick-paved circular driveway leading to a yellow five-story building with a one-level unit connected by a glassed-in walkway.

They circled around landscaped garden areas past the entrance and followed signs to a parking lot in the back. Passing familiar blood red anemones, radiant against dark shrubbery, Jack wondered how old the place was. Although it looked modern enough, its walls no doubt masked secrets from times of yore, as his mother would annoyingly say.

"Looks upscale for a nursing home," Jack said. "The old woman must be loaded."

Sherk chuckled. "Germany is very good to its senior citizens. Socialized health care strikes terror in the hearts of many Americans, but it works well here and in other European countries."

"Not gonna get into politics." Jack was aware of Sherk's socialist leanings, but right now, was too distracted to give a damn.

A few minutes later, his legs wobbled as they walked through the entry into a large, open lobby area smacking of German sterility. A young brown-haired woman sat at her computer behind a circular desk. She looked up, her straight teeth shining.

"Guten Tag, kann ich Ihnen helfen?"

Jack stood aside and let Sherk take over. "Ja, wir—"

The rest of the words were the usual muddle of rapid German, but Jack recognized "Ariana Gunther" in the midst.

The receptionist's upbeat expression faded as a frown appeared between her well-shaped eyebrows. She exchanged more conversation with Sherk. Although Jack couldn't understand the words, he sensed something was wrong. At one point, both the woman and Sherk glanced at him.

A couple minutes later, Sherk pointed Jack to a leather sofa in the spacious waiting area. "We'll sit over here and talk. There's a slight problem."

Chapter 8

Jack stared at him. "Why am I not surprised?"

"They won't let anyone see Ariana except family. I explained that you have a connection with her from the States, but the receptionist wouldn't budge; said it was against regulations to reveal anything, since we're not family."

Jack stared at Sherk. "Shit. Now what do we—"

"Hold on, there may be a solution. Turns out, the lady mentioned Ariana has a sister who lives in independent living unit. We could see her. Perhaps she knows what—"

"So, they have different units depending on how bad off you are." Jack recalled an aunt in the same situation.

Sherk nodded. "Right. They have different levels of supervision, so my guess is Ariana needs constant physical care or she has some form of dementia. But her sister, Renate, is right here. It'll only take minutes to walk there, and it's not a problem visiting her."

"Guess that's the only choice we have. Sure to be a crap shoot. Who knows if her sister ever met Pa back in the war?"

"I'd say there's a good chance, Jack. Sisters share secrets." Sherk said. "Let's go check it out."

They returned to the front desk and signed in to visit Renate Hahn. The receptionist pointed them in the appropriate direction, saying she'd call Frau Hahn and tell her to expect visitors.

Walking down the hall, Jack had the urge to bolt. Meeting Ariana's sister would be awkward. Thank God Sherk would do the talking. Definitely an advantage not speaking German.

"I dunno, Sherk, this is a long shot. I doubt she'll be able to help us with—"

"Hey, at least pretend the glass is half full. Don't give up. 'Hope is the thing with feathers.' "

"Not in the mood for Shakespeare."

"Emily Dickinson. She uses a bird as a metaphor for—"

"Yeah, I'm sure she does." Sherk was a pain in the ass sometimes. "Are we almost there?"

"Renate is in the adjoining wing across the way."

They reached the glassed-in walkway and headed for the independent living unit across a garden of greenery and more scarlet anemones. For someone who scoffed at fate and superstition, why did he have a vibe of eeriness? He tried to shake off the feeling. Besides, the complex was well-planned and tidy. For a nursing facility, this was as good as it got. In appearance anyway.

They entered a bright, open reception area, where Sherk approached an older man at a desk, who directed him to the location of Renate's apartment. Jack followed Sherk down a wide corridor that smelled of potpourri and Lysol. He was sure the florescent lighting illuminated beads of sweat forming on his forehead. A couple silver-haired ladies greeted them with "Guten Tag" as they passed a living room where more white or bald heads bent over cards or board games at small round tables. Why was everything white? Or red? He was being mocked by a façade of innocence. Muffled conversation and occasional titters floated in the air.

"This place is rockin'." Jack needed a little comic relief.

A door at the end of the hall was partially open. Sherk stopped. "This is it."

He tapped lightly and waited.

"Einen Moment bitte," a high, pleasant voice called out.

"Keine Eile," Sherk answered.

A delicate, birdlike woman opened the door further and beamed at Sherk. "Bitte kommen Sie herein." She beckoned the men to enter. As she glanced at Jack, her eyes narrowed, a hint of a frown between her eyebrows. He nodded at her in acknowledgment as she gave him a dove-like stare. Confused, he made an awkward step around her into the entry.

Sherk obviously noticed Renate Hahn's gaze. He took her hand and spoke in German for a couple minutes, uttering mysterious words beyond Jack.

The woman giggled nervously, placing her hand on her heart.

Jack wasn't sure how to react as he glanced around her uncluttered living room. He caught a whiff of gardenia and nostalgia in the air. A mahogany spinet piano sat in the corner with black and white photos in vintage silver frames atop its shiny surface.

Talking and smiling, Renate shooed them over to a plush burgundy sofa. Jack figured she had offered coffee or whatever was available. He could use a shot of Jameson about then.

"She's offering us coffee, tea, cakes, Jack. Want anything?"

"How 'bout whisky?" Sometimes it was an advantage when people didn't understand English.

Sherk groaned. "Afraid not. I'll decline coffee for both of us." He spoke to the woman, who nodded, chatted, and kept looking at Jack. She took a seat in an armchair close to Sherk and crossed her toothpick legs.

Jack noticed her bony knees under beige cotton pants. A red blouse highlighted her rosy cheekbones and dark lipstick. Her pale blue doe-like eyes were wide-set like Uma Thurman's. With her white blunt haircut, she was what his mother would call a well-preserved woman.

She and Sherk continued their conversation, including more stares at Jack. Nothing like sitting there while people talked about him in German.

Sherk turned to him. "She told us to call her 'Renate,' and said Ariana has lived in the memory care unit for about two years. She started declining quite a while ago, and Renate sees her almost every day. Ariana's husband died almost fifteen years ago; they had one daughter who visits now and then."

Jack nodded as he shifted in his seat, hoping Renate would quit staring at him.

"She remarked your eyes are familiar, but she can't place where she's seen you." Sherk turned to Jack. "I told her you look like an American actor and lots of folks notice it, but she doesn't know anybody like that."

"Does she get why we're here?"

"I'm gonna give her details now. I'll show her the letter too." Sherk leaned toward Renate and spoke. He removed the letter from his pocket and handed it to her. She reached for a pair of reading glasses on an end table and held the letter close to her face, reading her sister's words from long ago. Sherk helped her with the English terms.

She looked at Jack and gasped. Her right hand flew to her throat, eyes darting to the wall. After placing the letter on her lap, she removed her glasses and covered her eyes with her hands. She sniffled. "Mein Gott."

Sherk handed her a Kleenex. "Alles wird gut."

Renate took the tissue and dabbed her eyes. "Danke." She and Sherk exchanged more words as she held the letter as if it were an injured bird.

She stared at Jack, her blue eyes dinner plates.

"Oh mein Gott! Du hast seine Augen."

Sherk said, "She believes you have his eyes. Talking about your father. Did you look like him?"

Jack shrugged. "Hell, I dunno. I guess a little. Some people said us kids looked more like him than Ma." Goosebumps tingled on his arms.

Renate rose and stepped toward Jack, bending down as she eased herself between him and Sherk. She gently patted his cheeks and ears. Jack stiffened, but allowed her touch.

She turned to Sherk, went on speaking. "Mein Gott. Du siehst aus wie dein Vater. Wie John. Ach—"

"She keeps commenting you look like your dad," said Sherk.

Taken aback, Jack half-chuckled and nodded. Couldn't come up with anything else to do but sit and wait until Sherk took a break in his conversation to translate what the hell was going on.

After several minutes, Renate turned to Jack, leaned toward him, and kissed his cheek. He gave Sherk a helpless look. "How do I react?"

"Do nothing, Jack. She knows why we're here, and she and Ariana have always been close, including during the war. Renate got acquainted with your dad, and there's a long story which she'll save for another time."

"What about us meeting the Frau—Ariana?"

Sherk adjusted his glasses. "It's getting close to her dinner time. Renate usually joins her sister, so we can go along or wait till tomorrow morning. We're allowed to visit, since we're with Ariana's sister. What do you want to do?"

"As long as we're here, I vote let's go. We're on a roll, and I'm anxious to see Ariana, uh Gunther is it?"

"Yes. I'll tell Renate we'll meet her sister today. She's totally oblivious to everything, so no need to tell her we're coming. She wouldn't comprehend it anyway."

Ten minutes later, after walking through several halls and an activity room where small, wrinkled men and women painted their little wooden sailboats, Jack determined Renate was in damn good shape for the ripe old age of eighty-four. His curiosity piqued. He asked Sherk what more she'd told him, but no new details were offered. Jack was puffing when at last they reached a room with a laminated picture of a bright bluebird on the door above a nameplate which read 'Ariana Gunther'.

"Hallo, Hallo, Ari." Renate opened the door and peeked in. "Ach, ich —" she spoke as she walked into the room, motioning Jack and Sherk to follow.

A nurse's aide sat beside a silver-haired woman perched like a sparrow on the edge of her neatly-made bed. When she discerned Renate's voice, she looked up, raised her eyebrows, twitched her mouth at the corners. She wore a lavender blouse with lightweight dark pants. Jack noted the sisters' family resemblance, same wide-apart eyes, and although Ariana was three years older, she had an ageless, ethereal aura about her as if she guarded secrets of the universe. She held out a skeletal arm to Sherk, then to Jack. He bent closer. Her fine cheekbones and Cupid's bow lips reminded him of an aging Ingrid Bergman. She must've been a beauty when his old man met her.

The aide leaned close to Ariana, spoke to her softly, and left the room. Renate sat on the bed beside her sister, who continued to glance at her visitors, then her eyes stared straight ahead at nothing. Or everything.

Sherk and Renate talked to one another, while Ariana remained expressionless. Jack perked up when Renate said, "John Bailey" amongst the plethora of guttural words. Ariana jerked her head to the side, then silence.

The room was cheerful enough; one large space with a bath. No plants or objects adorned the small tables, but Jack noticed the same bluebird image attached on the door was repeated on a wall by a large window.

"Renate will show her the letter later," Sherk said, "even though it may not register. She'd like you to sit by Ariana, catch her eye, and say something, doesn't matter what. See if she reacts to the sound of your voice."

Jack felt like a fool, but acquiesced. He took Renate's place beside her sister, reached for her hands, and held them, catching a scent of rosewater and long-ago memories. He cleared his throat. Her eyes made contact with his before flickering away.

"Go ahead, Jack. Speak her name. See how she is."

"Okay, here goes. Hello, Ariana. How are you doing today?" Jack swallowed his words. He'd stepped outside of himself. "Are you ready for dinner soon?" Hell, when was he ever this nice?

He looked at Sherk. "Is that enough? She doesn't seem—"

Ariana let out a moan as she slowly turned to Jack. "Die Drossel. Die Drossel."

"What's she saying?" Jack gazed at her wide eyes.

"It sounds like 'the bluebird'. I have no idea what that's supposed to mean, except for the pictures she has." Sherk looked at Renate and questioned her. She didn't appear to understand why she'd utter the word, other than mentioning the bluebird had always been her sister's favorite.

Jack started to rise, but Ariana grasped his hand, pulling him back, her grip like a vise. "Die—die" her voice trailed off.

Renate spoke to Sherk, who said to Jack, "She wants you to stay by her."

Jack reluctantly sat back down. What he'd give for a shot of Jameson. He glanced at Sherk. "What did she tell you?"

"Renate can see by the way she's holding onto your hand. She's very agitated, but doesn't want you to leave." He listened while Renate spoke to him. "You triggered something in her, Jack. Does your voice sound like your father's?"

"Damned if I know. Never thought about it. Don't most men sound alike?"

Murmuring humming sounds like a bumblebee, Ariana gently rubbed his arm and hands. Her feline gaze unnerved him.

"Renate informs us dinner time is almost here. We can come back tomorrow morning, and she'll tell us Ariana's story." Sherk rose from his chair. "It's been an emotionally draining day for Renate meeting you and reliving part of their past. Many Germans won't talk about the war, but I explained to her why you and your brother want to understand more about your father's experience."

Leaning toward her sister, Renate gingerly pried Jack's hands away from Ariana's grasp. She spoke softly in German while Ariana carried on humming a melody known to her alone. Renate looked up at Sherk and spoke.

Jack stood slowly and waited for a break in their conversation. He wouldn't tell Sherk he was on pins and needles to find out about Ariana, and was hesitant to leave.

"Time to go. We'll come back tomorrow morning." Sherk led the way out the door.

"What did Renate just whisper?" Jack said as they headed down the corridor.

Sherk paused. "After all these years, the time has finally come to tell Ariana's story."

CHAPTER 9

At 10:00 the next morning, Jack and Sherk settled in on Renate Hahn's velvety couch after declining coffee and pastries. Jack's mouth was a cotton ball, so he told Sherk he'd like water. Renate seemed happy to oblige, and returned with three water glasses clinking on a silver tray.

Sherk stood, took the tray and placed it on the doily atop the rectangular oak coffee table, while Renate walked to the piano to retrieve several framed pictures. She slowly placed them in front of the men.

After easing herself onto a lavender brocade chair near Sherk, she handed him one of the photos, its silver frame, tarnished on the edges. As Renate spoke to Sherk, Jack leaned over and took in the black-and-white picture of a somber, but nice-looking family, the man and woman seated in tufted chairs surrounded by three children, and a baby reclining on its mother's lap. The woman wore a long, dark dress with puffed sleeves with a cameo brooch at her neck. Two boys, dressed in dark vests, suits, and bow ties, stood behind a little girl in a layered lace dress with a dropped waist. An oversized white bow rested on top of her straight pale hair. A light, flowing gown clothed the baby. A christening perhaps?

Sherk turned to Jack. "This is a portrait of the Schröder family. Renate is the baby, Ariana the girl, Fritz and Kurt, her older brothers, along with parents, Emil and Erna. They're all deceased except the sisters."

Jack noted a resemblance between the girls and their father, who boasted the same wide-set eyes. "Yeah, these pictures are like some of Ma's old family photos. All black and white and everyone looking sober."

Renate placed the picture on the table and handed another one to Sherk. She continued pointing at the photos. Jack thought he recognized

"Sie war zehn Jahre alt" and "Bund Deutscher Mädel" amongst the rapid-fire words. Sounded familiar.

Two young girls in the next photo beamed at Jack, one with blond braids, the other's hair a shade darker, cut short and blunt. Standing side by side on a porch step of a modest, light-colored house, they wore identical uniforms of white blouses, long neckties, and dark skirts. Both held up small swastika flags. The girls, fresh-faced and the picture of innocence.

Jack's jaw clenched at the sight, but he resisted the urge to speak aloud. He noticed lush flowering bushes flanking the steps next to the flags. Besides the girls, a sinister contrast not lost on him.

Sherk said, "I'm sure you guessed the girls are Ariana and Renate around ages ten and thirteen in this picture. They joined the German League of Girls, which was the female counterpart of the Hitler Youth. Renate said their father was against their enlisting, but more of that later."

Jack grimaced. "Gives ya the chills just to look at them. Those happy faces. Didn't have a clue what the flags really meant."

Sherk spoke to Renate and then turned to Jack. "Their brother, Kurt, took the picture. He was in the Youth, and argued a lot with their father over it."

Jack shook his head. "God, can't imagine what they went through."

"Me neither. Sometime I'll tell you what little I've gleaned from my relatives. Not much though. Their lips are sealed."

Renate showed them several more family photos, all fascinating to Jack in an uncanny way. These people could've been his relatives. Except his never lived under the Third Reich. What shadows hid behind the pleasant veneer on the Schröders' faces? What did they know? Or not know?

After Renate returned the pictures to the piano, she sat again, sipped her water, and kept speaking to Sherk. "Sind Sie so weit?"

He turned to Jack. "She's ready to tell us Ariana's story. But she wants us to be patient because it'll take awhile. She may need a break now and then."

"Okay. Are you gonna stop her every few minutes to translate?"

Sherk nodded. "Yeah, I'll see what works best. If it gets too intense, I'll let her go on and not interrupt. I'll tell you later."

Jack's pulse raced. He took a gulp of water. Was he ready for whatever this tiny woman would reveal about his old man? Wonder if he did something in the war. Something underhanded? Jack wondered why that idea popped into his head.

Sherk went on. "Renate also said that in order for you to understand what your father saw and did back then, you need to understand Ariana and their family."

"Okay." Jack loosened his collar. Might as well try and relax. Might take a while.

"And she swore us to secrecy."

Jack was puzzled. "Wonder why. People realize what went on back then, what the Nazis did."

"It seems more private than the war issues, so I promised everything she said would be confidential."

Jack leaned back, attempting to make himself comfortable. Renate gave him a Mona Lisa smile. What was her big secret? Why would it still matter?

Chapter 10
Renate – near Munich, 1930s

You may wonder why I'm about to tell our family's story, and not just Ariana's. I must tell you because the war changed us. It changed John Bailey. How could it be otherwise?

I've never told another living soul. But I must. I must for Ariana's sake. And for John's as well. For his sons. So they can truly understand him, what he witnessed.

Our awareness of impending evil began with Papa. Then our friends. Then the schools. Then the girls camp. We were living under a deepening shadow. But we didn't notice.

We were the Schröders, an ordinary German family, two boys, two girls, Papa a dentist. We lived near Munich in the peaceful village of Dachau. Our house was a gray brick bungalow with white trim, five steps to the porch spanning the front of the house. Small by today's standards

Flowers bloomed in every yard on our street. Oh, the blue cornflowers were exquisite. And the lilacs; I can still smell their fragrance by the porch. Mutti loved the blossoms and greenery, but Frau Hilda did most of the gardening.

Mutti studied piano at the University of Music and Performing Arts and played with the Munich Philharmonic before marrying Papa. He said she was never the same after having children and leaving the orchestra. I later understood what he meant.

I can still see her sitting in the parlor at her piano. She'd play Beethoven's sonatas by the hour. Number Eight and Opus Thirteen haunt me to this day. Frau Hilda cooked and cleaned for us. She was a widow who needed a place to stay.

My brother Fritz was the oldest, then Kurt. Ariana was born in 1925, and I came along three years later. We all had fair hair, the boys were hazel-eyed like Mutti, Ariana and I with Papa's blue eyes. But Fritz was different. Papa and Mutti would tell us to leave him alone, to ignore him. It was hard to do when he yelled if we touched him. He rocked back and forth a lot. *He can't help it. It's a sickness.* He was ten years older than me, but he didn't go to school with us.

Papa told us fairy tales at bedtime, but Fritz couldn't sit and pay attention. He made strange sounds like quacking or barking, so he went with Mutti in her room. Like most German children, Ariana, Kurt, and I listened to the horror tales of Struwwelpeter. I can still recite *Pauline and the Matches…. but Pauline said, oh, what a pity, for when they burn it is so pretty…*

Years later, I realized Papa read the tales to teach us lessons. Not only the obvious, to obey our parents or we'd burn up like Pauline did, but subtle messages. Don't be tempted by what sounds or looks good. Be careful. Careful of matches, the woods, and gingerbread houses.

Yes, our childhood was ordinary to me, because that's what I grew up with. Mutti had her headaches and would disappear in her room for hours. Frau Hilda watched Fritz most every day until he was older. We grew up that way, like everyone else. We thought.

Looking back, though, we missed the signs.

My best friend, Judith, lived down the block in a big two-story home. We played with our dolls, went on picnics, swam, and rowed in her father's boat on the lake. Her dolls were nicer than mine; Ariana and I had one Kestner porcelain doll, but Judith had five. Her little Spitz dog named Heidi looked like a fox with long golden fur around her sharp little face. Ariana and I loved playing chase with her, Judith's mother yelling not to run in the house. I begged for a dog, but Mutti poo-pooed it. *Quit pestering me, Renate. You children are enough for me to bear.*

Judith's father was our doctor until one day Papa said we needed to find a new one. *But why can't we keep going to Dr. Friedman?* I don't recall what Papa and Mutti responded, but after that, Dr. Schmidt became our doctor. His office was farther away, and smaller. Mutti complained that we had to ride the bus to see him, since we didn't have a car yet. If we were too sick, then he made a house call. But we still played with Judith, so I didn't think much about it.

Until later.

Chapter 11

I remember Papa and Mutti arguing about things I didn't understand. They would bicker with Kurt sometimes too. Papa would go out in the evenings to meetings, he'd claim. At the time I thought our family was normal, except Fritz. He was often the subject of quarrels between my parents, and when Kurt got older and joined the Youth, he'd horn in on their disagreements. Sometimes our neighbor, Walter Gunther and his papa would come over to talk privately with Papa. Walter was older than Kurt, and he and Papa seemed to agree on things. I could tell that Walter was sweet on Ariana.

She and I asked many questions about why Fritz had to be careful of playing outdoors with us, but Papa would never answer. Probably because last month Fritz ran away and hid in the neighbor's dog house until dark. *You girls don't need to worry; we'll take care of it; everything will be fine. Fritz is different than you, but we love him the same. We want to keep him safe from certain people.*

Things got more confusing because of the secrets Kurt would tell us. *Renate, don't tell anyone, especially Papa. He thinks the Führer is wrong.* Ariana and I promised we wouldn't tell, so Kurt told us things his school teachers said that we hadn't been taught yet. He said the Untermensch were inferior and we needed to stay away from them until they were gone. They would ruin the German people because they were born damaged and not true Germans. *Some of them were even in school. Last week a Roma boy had his head measured at school to see if he was pure, but we knew that he wasn't a real German.*

Ariana said she wasn't aware of that and how was Kurt convinced of these things? Sometimes we got tired of his talking and went back to playing. Besides, I didn't like keeping secrets from Papa.

Looking back on those years, it didn't happen all at once. Like someone said, farmers don't watch their corn growing, but they know it does. Then one day, it's over their heads.

· · · · ·

You might assume the years before and during the first part of the war were terrible for Germany, but for us, we always had enough food, clothes, and toys. I don't recall having to scrimp. By the time I was six or seven, people got jobs and weren't hungry any more. Teachers, store clerks, everyone except Papa would pronounce: *The Führer is our savior. He gave people food again, put them back to work, Germany's new order. We have pride once more.*

From the time he turned six, Kurt was active in a boys' youth group, like Boy Scouts. Fritz couldn't handle organized activities, so he attended a special school for a while. But he would still scream if we touched his tin soldiers lined in a row. I was a little kid when he was around, so I don't recall much until later when he was sent away for good.

I was only five when the Führer came to power. Later I learned the boys' groups were dissolved and the Hitler Youth took over. Kurt was twelve and excited to join and wear the uniform and be part of the new Germany. He argued with Papa about joining, but after a while things settled down. Several years later, membership in the Youth was mandatory for all Aryans, but of course, Fritz couldn't join. He would go to a camp for a few days and then come back, but he never got to be normal.

In fact, Dr. Schmidt talked with Mutti and Papa about sending Fritz to Lucerne so he could stay in a sanitarium. But Mutti didn't want to break up the family, so she and Papa had long debates about what to do. At the time I didn't understand about Fritz and the real reason Dr. Schmidt and Papa wanted to send him away. Ariana thought they were being mean, but we learned the truth later.

· · · · ·

So life drifted on, and we were ordinary like everyone else, other than Fritz. I was the last one in our family to start school. We walked there with Mutti or Frau Hilda, and along the way we'd stop for Judith. In school, I remember a large portrait of the Führer hung in each classroom with the red and black flag. I learned to read, and we studied laws about our country, particularly keeping us pure Aryans. Our room had a big map in front. The teacher let us stick pins on it to mark the front lines after the war started.

The next year Judith couldn't go to school any more. No one told me why, but when Kurt wanted to tell me, Papa shushed him. But I still played with her sometimes when Mutti had headaches.

And then that summer, I was no longer allowed to play with Judith.

Mutti said her family wasn't a good influence, whatever that meant. Besides, she wasn't allowed to go to any parks or lakes anymore. She'd just started to ride her new red bicycle when it was taken away. I could not understand why Judith was different from us. Ariana and I bothered our parents with lots of questions, but they never gave us a much of an answer.

Papa just looked sad. *I'm sorry, girls, the world isn't safe for Judith, or for you if you're with her. It's not fair. I hope her family can go somewhere safe before too long.*

Ariana said even though Judith would ruin the German blood, she wasn't like the rest of them our teachers warned us about. Judith was normal, like us.

What became of her? Perhaps it's better not to know.

CHAPTER 12
Weimar

Renate took a sip of water, eased herself from the chair, and stretched. "Ich werde uns Kaffee holen."

Sherk offered to help her with coffee, but Renate shooed him away and headed for the kitchen.

Jack stood and yawned. "That was quite a spiel. You ready to tell me what she said?"

"Yeah." Sherk bent his neck, gazing toward the kitchen. "She'll be busy making coffee for a few minutes." Sherk pointed to the piano. "That was their mother's, who studied music at university; it sounds like she could've been a concert pianist. But marriage and kids put an end to that."

"Guess ya can't have everything. Surprised I understood a few names here and there, like Kurt and Fritz."

"Ja, before long, you'll be fluent in German." Sherk retrieved the family pictures from the piano and brought them to the sofa. "You can kind of see that Fritz is a little different, after what Renate said. A tough situation, especially back then."

Jack flopped down and peered at the photo. "What's the problem with him?"

"Let me bring you up to speed." Sherk summarized the information Renate revealed, emphasizing her insistence the Schröders were everyday citizens, living a decent life in a small town. "As for Fritz, I'd guess he had autism or ADHD. You may presume autism wasn't labeled back then, but a Swiss psychiatrist used the term in the early 1900's." Sherk cleared his throat. "I'm guessing Fritz's parents were afraid he'd end up in the T-4 program, which—"

"The what?"

Sherk glanced toward the kitchen. "Hate to talk about this, but when the war started, the Nazis were determined to get rid of people who were unfit, like the chronically sick or disabled, both mentally and physically. Their notion to attain a pure race. So, Renate's parents wanted to hide Fritz away in Switzerland so he'd be safe."

A chill ran through Jack. "So, what happened to the kid?" He was familiar with the despicable Nazi decree, but hadn't known its name.

"Nothing's been said. Haven't reached that part of the story."

"Unser Kaffee und Kuchen." Renate chirped as she glided into the room holding a silver tray, tarnished in one corner. It looked heavier than she was.

Sherk rose, took the tray and placed it on the coffee table. Whiffs of cinnamon and apple floated in the room like a gentle breeze. He carefully placed three china plates covered with golden strudel beside the tray, along with shiny forks and flowery cloth napkins.

"Greift zu!" Renate indicated white dainty cups of steamy coffee.

Why did women have to fuss over food? When it came to grub, presentation was way over-rated. Jack would be happy to scarf down the pastry with his hands. Why drag out the good china and silverware? Typical of women in that generation, he guessed.

They settled on the sofa. Renate and Sherk added sugar cubes and cream to their coffee and stirred it with tiny silver spoons.

Jack took a bite of warm strudel. "Mmm. How do you translate 'delicious' in German?"

"Sehr lecker."

Repeating the words, Jack nodded at Renate and grinned. She thanked him, her blue eyes glimmering. She seemed pleased he made an effort in pronunciation.

Sherk proceeded to pepper Renate with questions, and he in turn translated answers to Jack.

"What about Judith's family?" Jack said. "I get they were Jews, but I thought doctors couldn't practice at all."

"After a while, Jewish doctors were forbidden to have Aryan patients. Jews were banned from medical, dental, and law schools, but doctors still saw patients on the sly later on."

Jack shook his head. "What about Fritz?"

Sherk straightened his glasses. "Like I suspected, he had some form of autism, and the older he got, the harder it was for the parents to conceal his problem without isolating him. Renate will tell the rest of his story later."

After finishing their coffee and strudel, Sherk offered to clear the table, so he and Jack returned the tray and dishes to the small, tidy kitchen.

Back in the living room, Renate was ready to tell them more, but she informed Sherk it would take one or two more days to finish the story.

"Must be some saga," Jack said. He hoped her family had been spared at least some terrors of the war. How did things end for Ariana? Their father? Fritz?

Renate smoothed her silvery hair and sank into the soft brocade chair. Through the window, sunshine created a veil of light on a potted floor plant, turning its leaves vibrant green and casting long shadows on the hardwood floor.

"Fühlt euch wie zuhause." She cleared her throat and began to speak.

CHAPTER 13
Renate – 1930s

What do I know about memory? When you become old and used up like me, it's easy to allow the past to take over. Some memories are sharp as teeth, others like gauzy clouds floating in your brain. Others flutter around like a trapped moth; others are right on the edge of remembrance. Like a familiar melody you can't identify. And it's only now, years later, that I recognize these scenes of the past for what they were. So, I grasp onto the good memories for dear life. As for Ariana, who can tell where her mind takes her now. I'm sure she's happy enough, wherever she is.

I told you about Fritz and then Judith. In time, more decrees against the Jews came out, and then things got worse. I begged Papa to let Judith come and hide in our house. *Oh, please, please, Papa, she can stay with me and Ariana. We have room. And Heidi the dog, could stay too.*

The sorrow of the world was etched on his face. How to make us comprehend?

In another year or two, Ariana and I joined the BDM, or the Band of German Maidens, which you recall was the female branch of the Hitler Youth. Of course, Papa and Mutti argued bitterly over this, and he eventually agreed our family would be safer if we joined. It must have broken his heart, but he didn't want to draw attention to us. You see, our father's beliefs were different from our teachers' lessons on racial hygiene, which caused him to fight with Mutti and Kurt. It was hard for Ariana to keep her opinions to herself because she had a mind of her own. But she was smart enough to take Papa's advice. *Until this is over, girls, we need to live in a world of silence and secrets.*

Yes, silence and secrets. All of Germany lived those words. They are forever engraved in my brain. In my soul too, because I loved Papa. But we usually enjoyed our time in the BDM. We got to wear uniforms like

50

you saw in the photo, and we played sports, did gymnastics, enjoyed camping and swimming and canoeing. We'd sit around the campfire singing patriotic songs. It wasn't all fun though. When we were older, we learned how to sew, cook, and make beds. Ariana and I hated that. But we had to grow up to be the best German wives we could and have a lot of children. Oh yes, we were also taught to stay away from people who were different from us, like Jews and people with darker skin, especially boys, so they couldn't do things to German girls to make babies. Ha! Ariana and I secretly made fun of all that. One of our leaders was a huge woman with a granite face. *You must avoid racial defilement at all costs.* Ariana said that surely anyone would avoid that woman.

One day Papa sat me and Ariana down when I was ten or so, and told us he was in the Social Democratic party, which was not the party of Hitler. He told us his views in simple terms, how dangerous racial hatred was, but he pounded into us that we must not talk about his ideas and opinions to anyone, not our friends, teachers, anyone. He reminded us of the Struwwelpeter tale of "Hans Look in the Air", how we need to be on guard at all times. I remember to this day, *Hans looking at the sky and the clouds that floated by – once he walked beside the river, one step more, oh sad to tell – headlong in poor Hans fell.*

Shortly after that, the Gunthers next door came over, and Herr Gunther was all excited about something. He and Walter looked so worried, I was afraid. Mutti wanted me and Ariana to go to our room, but Ariana said she was old enough to listen to things. Usually we were punished if we didn't obey, but the grownups were too distracted to care. They talked about how Jewish stores and synagogues were burned and smashed up all over Germany. A lot of Jews were taken away to prison or even killed. Later Kurt told us that Hitler didn't condone the violence, that they were just groups of street thugs that were causing all the damage.

And now, memory becomes hazy. The years blend together like watercolors on paper. But all of the horror wasn't covert. It was hiding in plain sight, under our noses, like the day a policeman shoved Mr. Aarons out of his butcher shop, yelling "filthy rodent" at him.

If Papa had joined the Party, our family would have fared better. But he had to follow his conscience. Ariana used to comment he was too nice a man for his own good. She may have repeated it from Mutti, who wasn't like Papa. Oh, she had mental problems, but children don't catch onto such things as melancholy until years later. Mutti should have been a pianist in an orchestra, but then Ariana and I may not have happened.

•   •   •   •   •

We vaguely became aware of doom around the edges of our lives. During those times, Papa spent more and more evenings away, and many of his patients left him for other dentists. The Fischers and Leibmanns were forced to leave, but Kurt said others deserted him because Papa wasn't loyal to the Party. Meanwhile, bit by bit our neighbors would tell stories, but we saw things too. We'd walk past empty storefronts, delicatessens, dress shops with new owners. Judith's house looked vacant, and then one day two strange boys played ball in the front yard. Ariana asked Papa where the Friedmans were, and to this day I remember his answer. *It's best we don't know such things, Ariana. We hope they are safe wherever they are.*

•   •   •   •   •

And then it happened. Sitting in the parlor before bedtime one night, we jumped at the sound of brakes squealing and car doors slamming in front. Papa walked to the window and peeked through the curtains. Shoulders drooped, he scuffled to the door and opened it. Two surly-looking men in long black coats spoke in muffled tones and stepped inside. Papa talked in a low voice.

He and Kurt expected it to happen; they just didn't know when. Papa trudged to his room along with one of the hatchet-faced men, while the other one stood watching us. No one spoke.

A couple minutes later, they returned, Papa carrying his small, worn leather suitcase. *They're taking me in for questioning, maybe for a couple days. Don't worry, I'll be home soon.*

He hugged Mutti and kissed us goodbye. The men nodded at us, and I watched Papa smile and march out the door like he was going on vacation.

Later Mutti commented how calm the policemen were. *We were lucky they didn't tear the house apart. And how polite they were to me and you children. Who'd have thought?*

We never saw Papa again.

A week later we were told that Papa was taken to the Munich Prison located at Gestapo Headquarters in the former Wittelsbacher Palace. He was detained for several days and then transported to the detention center built five or six years ago from an old munitions factory at the edge of Dachau, our once-lovely, quiet village.

So, we carried on without Papa. Frau Hilda took over the household while Mutti gradually faded further into herself. Our Opa, Emil, Papa's father, often helped us out. He and Oma lived in Munich, and sometimes Fritz stayed with them for a few days, since he was happy at their house.

After months floated by, we quit badgering Mutti about when Papa would come home. We were busy at school and the BDM. But Ariana didn't accept everything our teachers and leaders taught us because Papa had told us many times about the difference between facts and opinions. Papa was gone, but he left his warnings behind for us. We kept our thoughts to ourselves and said nothing about our father's beliefs. As for Mutti, she played the piano hour after hour, lost in her world of Beethoven.

All I can comment once again, is the horror was stealthy, like a fog rolling in. Most of us turned a blind eye at the violence, the smashing of store windows by street thugs we thought were not under Hitler's orders. Besides, his dreams for a new Germany promised intelligent, healthy citizens. And many saw nothing wrong with taking back territories that belonged to the Fatherland. On September first of 1939, our friends and neighbors welcomed the news of Germany's invasion of Poland. Our teachers told us that Polish land was really on German soil. We needed to take back what was rightfully ours.

Ah, the power of propaganda.

•   •   •   •   •

Now, I'm afraid I must stop and bid you goodbye until tomorrow. It tires me out telling our story, but the time has come to bring it out from the shadows and into the light.

Chapter 14
Renate – 1939-1940s

Good morning to you, Herr Sherk and Herr Jack. Hopefully, you had a restful evening and a big breakfast at the Leonardo. You chose a good hotel. Perhaps you two will have time to see Goethe's garden home and the Schloss Weimar.

I had a nice evening with Ariana. We ate our usual dinner together, and I told her about your visit, talking about our family. Her eyes widened when I mentioned John Bailey's name. She stared at me and said, "Yes, yes." But she often mumbles that, so who knows, but she indicated she understood on some level.

Meeting you two nice men has brought a change in my life. Stirring up memories from another world, so long ago. I'm not sure of the word, but it's like I have unburdened myself. And I am lighter somehow. Oh, what's the word?

Ah, yes, a catharsis. Of course, many Germans refuse to talk of those years. Too painful for some, and guilt and denial for others. People blame us, but in the end, what could we have done? Even if we had known the horrors of the camps, what were we women and children and people like Papa to do? I'd like the answer. He stood up for his beliefs, he wouldn't join the Party. Look what happened to him. Did he save any lives or help the greater good? I question you again. What could we have done? Please pardon my emotion. It gets the better of me sometimes.

•   •   •   •   •

Now we're settled with coffee, so once again we'll return to the beginning of the war. Yesterday I told you when it started, people weren't surprised. Our teachers were happy about taking Poland back, and of course I was just a young girl, and didn't understand what was going on. Ariana and I kept on with our BDM meetings, and Kurt was gone a lot in the Youth. I assured myself wherever Papa was, he would be against Germany's invasion of Poland.

So, life carried on without much change, except we missed our father. But in spite of that, we had fun times. Ariana and I loved going to the pictures, mostly musical comedies. Leny Marenbach was our favorite star. Ah, we wanted to be like her. Our BDM troop marched in parades, and one time they took a trip to Nuremburg for a big rally. Mutti and Frau Hilde said we couldn't go, we were too young, but Kurt did, which was so unfair because we had to stay home.

Mutti and our grandparents argued a lot about what to do with Fritz. She refused to send him away. Kurt told us about the T-4 plan where the government wanted to rid the German nation of undesirables, people unfit to carry on the Aryan race. Ariana and I cried and screamed at Kurt that they couldn't take our brother away, but he said Fritz should go into hiding in Switzerland so he'd be saved. To this day, I'm not sure if Kurt might have secretly been convinced his brother should be killed for the sake of the Fatherland, but he must've wished the best for Fritz, since he wanted him safe. With Papa gone, at least we didn't have to listen to him and Kurt argue about politics and who was right.

One night, Dr. Schmidt came to our house and talked privately with Mutti and Frau Hilde about Fritz. After the doctor left, Kurt, who had eavesdropped through the keyhole, took me and Ariana into his room and closed the door. Even though Kurt was mean to us at times, he wanted us to be aware of what was going on. His voice dropped to a near whisper. *Dr. Schmidt is ordered to turn in names of his patients who are unfit for the Aryan race, to keep Germany pure. That means handicapped people in wheelchairs and people like Fritz. He told Mutti to take Fritz to the sanitarium in Switzerland right now before it's too late.*

Fearful for Fritz's fate, Mutti ultimately agreed to send him to Switzerland. All I remember is the next day Opa drove to our house and Frau Hilde hurried Fritz into the car. We only had time for a quick hug goodbye. Mutti was crying and grabbing onto him as Opa and Kurt peeled him away from her grasping arms. Ignoring her and very excited, Fritz chattered on about taking a train trip with Opa, but of course he had no idea where he'd end up. We were aware of the truth. He was sent to Lucerne to a special home for people like him.

For the next several years of the war, our BDM troop worked for the German effort. At first, we wrote letters to the troops, knitted wool gloves and socks, even made straw slippers for soldiers in hospitals. Kurt was trained to be an air raid warden, which was an essential job as Allied bombings on the larger German cities increased.

Ariana and I volunteered as Red Cross nurse's aides in the Schwabinger Krankenhaus in Munich. During the week, we stayed with our grandparents, whose large apartment was only a few blocks away. We walked back and forth from hospital, except when it got dark and Opa picked us up in his car.

Looking back, the years all blended together. But gradually, optimism, spirit, and what is it called, ah, national pride faded. People's faces looked downcast, gloomy. Shouts of victory grew dim, replaced with silence. The raids and destruction escalated. All of Munich seemed to turn gray. The sirens wailed their anguish, then we'd scurry to the underground shelter, huddle close with Oma and Opa, the odor of human waste assaulting our nostrils. Soon strangers became friends, all of us bonded together by one cause: survival. The cries of babies and terrified children clinging to their haggard, fearful mothers still haunt me to this day.

Mutti begged us to come home to Dachau because the bombing wasn't as bad in our village, so we agreed, and stayed with her and Frau Hilde for a month or so. We never saw Kurt, and no one was sure where he was, which caused Mutti to wring her hands in despair. Ariana and I missed Fritz and prayed for his safety. We were Catholic, but hadn't been to Mass for years. Walter Gunther came around wanting to be with Ariana, but she wasn't too interested. He'd taken a shine to her years before. A nice person, but she liked him in a brotherly way.

We stayed in the house, knitting and sewing for the soldiers, but it was boring. Ariana said as nurses, we did much more good for the war effort.

One day a leader from the BDM knocked on the door. She told us to return to the Munich hospital because things were getting worse for the Reich, and our girls' youth organization was falling apart. *They need you ladies, all of us, young and old. More of our soldiers are coming from the east — Stalingrad, Smolensk, they're broken, frostbitten. Ach, Frau Schröder, you must allow your girls to serve the Fatherland.*

So Mutti reluctantly let us return to Munich and the hospital. We took care of many more patients than before, and we were given more responsibility, the same as real nurses. We had to change dressings on bloody, open wounds, and other things I hate to mention. Ariana, perhaps because she was older, had more of a stomach for it than me. *Oh Renate, you'll get used to it. We all have blood and innards.* At first, I ran to the toilets to be sick, but later not as much.

But it took a toll on us. We witnessed grizzly sights of burns, amputations, more. One night Ariana called me to help her with a poor soldier just brought in. Gott im Himmel, his insides were outside his stomach, his soiled hands moving upward on his sides, as if he was trying to press it all in. It looked like a family of bloody snakes curled around each other over his torso. Ariana's arms were bathed in red. She tried to hold his shoulders down. And the stench. Like sewage with an odd tinge of almond. Oh, why did I look? The poor man couldn't stand the searing pain, and screamed, begged us to kill him. My eyes floated to the ceiling. I was lightheaded. Blackness surrounded me.

When I came to, Ariana and Stefan, our burly medic friend, knelt beside me on the floor, and helped me sit up. The soldier still yelled piteously, *Gott, lass mich gehen.*

Ariana led me to a corner where I sat in a chair, my head in my hands. *It's okay, Renate. He's in septic shock. He won't last much longer.*

I've never spoken of that poor soldier begging for the mercy of death. Someone's son, his mother like Mutti perhaps. Or perhaps he was a husband, a young father? And he was just one. One of thousands.

During the last fall and winter of the war, rumors were rampant about Germany losing ground, and people weren't sure our country would become ruler of all Europe. Air raids intensified, and the city turned into sooty rubble. The food shortage worsened, with rations severely cut. Women waited in long queues winding around blocks from the marketplace, hoping for a loaf of stale bread, eggs, biscuits, or whatever was left. Several women brought stools to sit on as they waited. Ariana and I longed for Frau Hilde's roast beef, potato dumplings, Apfelkuchen, but those days were gone. The only available meat was bully beef, like corned beef, which we got sick and tired of. Neither Ariana nor I ever cooked or ate that beef again.

More folks tried to escape to the country, and once again, Mutti begged us to leave the hospital and come home to Dachau. Stefan announced that the Allies invaded Germany on the Western Front. *They crossed the Rhine, occupied Düsseldorf, Cologne, heading for the Ruhr area, to shut off communications. Ach Gott, they're going to take the Rhineland before long.* Stefan babbled on about tanks, General Bradley. I thought he'd never hush up.

By March of 1945 most city streets were piles of wreckage and rising dust from the bombs. Opa could no longer drive to Mutti's, so we were forced to stay put in Munich. Businesses and government alike were unravelling, and Ariana said it was like we were on another planet with no rules. What's the word? Anarchy, yes, that's it.

People walked about in a daze. Some lived in the bombed-out shells of their former homes, the water either contaminated or turned off in many areas, and power outages were widespread. They used generators at the hospital. You'd see women and old men on the streets, cooking over open fires, trying to boil water. Our noses got used to the smoky stench wherever we found ourselves. Mothers tried to force stinky diluted soup made of rutabagas down their children. To this day, I can't look at rutabagas at the market, much less eat them.

I've blotted out memories of the final weeks of the war; just flashes of scenes now and then pop up. Ariana remembered more of our time with the sick and wounded, her memory once sharp. Sadly, a far cry from today.

A young soldier she took care of fell in love with her and begged her to marry him. Field doctors had amputated his right leg a week before he came in on a stretcher. The wound festered, and Ariana willingly tended to him. I couldn't bear the sight or putrid smell, but she was older than me, more grown up.

She gently told him they couldn't marry, not because of the leg, but she already had a beau. That wasn't true, even though Walter Gunther was sweet on her. You see, men were attracted to Ariana. She looked like an American movie star, I don't recall the name, with her creamy skin, wide-set sapphire eyes and ash blond hair parted on one side, the other swept down in a pageboy. Me, I was all right, but not the beauty Ariana was. In time, she discovered being beautiful back then could be a curse.

Those days reminded me of another fairy tale, "Flying Robert", a boy who disobeyed his parents and went out in a rainstorm. The wind caught his red umbrella. *Now look at him, silly fellow, Up he flies To the skies. No one heard his screams and cries… Only this one thing is plain, Rob was never seen again!*

The Struwwelpeter stories Papa told us years ago have embedded themselves in my mind.

Many times he had warned us to stay inside after dark, especially when the world around us turned perilous. But in those chaotic times, rules and habits shifted, disappeared, nothing the same. Toward the end, it was every man for himself, except for those with families. Ariana and I spent many hours at the hospital, and after work we'd walk to Opa's place, sometimes after dark.

Exhausted, Ariana said we needed to keep helping the sick and wounded, even though doctors and nurses were quitting the hospital, abandoning the sinking ship. Stefan said he had nowhere to go. *We must stay here, Ariana. They need our help and it gives us something to hang onto. A reason to keep living. We mustn't lose hope.*

•   •   •   •   •

I don't remember the exact date it happened, but rumors were flying around the hospital that day. Chaos erupted all over Munich. We were gulping down a lunch of bread and bacon we'd snuck from the kitchen when the doors flung open. Several policemen barreled inside shouting dire warnings. *Prisoners escaped from the BMW plant, they're on the loose. Be careful. They hate all Germans, no one's safe.*

We realized POW's were used as forced labor in factories, but we never sensed danger until then. One red-faced officer flailed his arms helplessly. *Guards are evacuating people at work camps all over the country, want to hide evidence, everyone fleeing right and left, no law and order.*

Panic stricken, Ariana gripped my arm. *"Renate, I've got to go check on Oma and Opa. You stay here where it's safe. I'll be back soon."*

"Wait, we can call the landlord – " I'd forgotten telephones had long-ago quit working. *"I'll go with you."*

"No, I can go faster alone. I know a short cut. You stay and help. You're needed here."

Before I could speak, Ariana ran off, racing past patients, nurses, equipment, and out the door.

Stefan told me not to worry, that Ariana was tougher than she looked.

Of course, I was aware of that, but I was jumpy and nervous about her out there running around alone. I dropped a bed pan, made a fine mess of it, no sooner cleaned it up and I spilled much-needed cough syrup down a little boy's chin. Fewer soldiers came in the hospital, but there were more women, children, and elderly needing treatment for bomb injuries, not to mention dysentery, impetigo, scabies.

Children cried, women moaned, all needing care. But I only thought of Ariana alone in a world of turmoil. Wondering why she hadn't returned, I asked Stefan what time it was. He assured me that only a couple hours had passed, she'd be back soon. How I wish he had been right.

CHAPTER 15
Weimar

Jack noticed Renate's lips quivering as she stared at the floor. He glanced at Sherk. "Does she need a break?"

"Most likely. I'll check." Sherk leaned toward Renate and spoke. She answered, her voice fluttering, soft as a feather. He turned to Jack.

"Renate's reaching a painful part in the story, and would like a short rest. But she wants us to stay. She'll go to her room and catch up on phoning her sewing group, so I'll update you on the story so far."

Both men stood and stretched. Renate offered more coffee and sweets which they declined, and she brushed Sherk's hand aside when he reached for the tray. Still shaken, she returned the dishes to the kitchen, the tray trembling, cups and plates nervously clinking until their harrowing journey drew to a close. On the way to her bedroom, she gave a quick wave to the men as she departed on little bird feet.

The sun had disappeared, stealing the brightness from the living room. Jack wandered to the piano, polished to a sheen, and studied the Schröder family photos again. His eyes settled on Fritz, staring into space, eyes vacant. Jack hoped the kid survived.

He flopped on the sofa, pulled out his phone, and read his messages. "Nothing earthshaking. A text from Jenny mentioning Ma hopes I'm getting enough to eat. Where am I? Cub Scout camp?" He sighed. "And Tommy wants an update on the Ariana story, so I'll email him tonight."

Sherk sat down, and eased his gangly legs under the coffee table.

"How much longer will it take Renate to finish the whole story?" Jack jiggled his foot.

"Hard to determine. She stopped right before the end of the war."

For the next hour, Sherk summarized Renate's story, stopping now and then to clarify details.

Jack kept silent, his anger sparking when Sherk mentioned the fate of Fritz.

"It still blows my mind how those bastards murdered little kids who were handicapped or mentally disabled or so-called impure German people." He again glanced toward the picture of Fritz. "Especially when it's somebody so close and personal."

"Yeah, the T-4 plan officially lasted until 1941 when Hitler publicly put a halt to it. It was an open secret, and a lot of citizens objected." Sherk cleared his throat. "But it was sustained in a more concealed manner and lasted till the end of the war. They gassed or euthanized not only the mentally and physically ill, but elderly patients as well. Renate didn't mention that, but she must now be aware."

Jack shook his head in disgust. "So Fritz was sent to Switzerland. Did he survive?"

"Renate didn't comment, but according to my previous research, he lived to his forties, and the documents also said Kurt died in his sixties."

Sherk carried on with more details, and was nearing the end when Jack interrupted.

"So in March of '45 the Allies invaded Germany. Wonder if Pa was involved in that. He refused to talk about the war except when he was drunk, and then his words didn't make sense. Damn, wish I would've quizzed my uncles more about it when they were still alive. They said his regiment reached Dachau, but there were several other units too."

"I'm not certain where his division came from." Sherk adjusted his glasses. "Possibly from the invasions on the Rhine crossings. Let's see how it plays out according to Renate."

Several minutes later, Sherk ended the story, indicating Ariana ran off alone in the streets to check on her grandparents.

"So these escaped prisoners, who were they? You said POW's."

"They were slave laborers used in factories like BMW and work camps, the euphemism for concentration camps. There were different levels and classifications of workers, mainly Poles worked in the Munich factories. The last few days of the war, people recognized Germany was losing, and everything fell apart."

"Can't imagine our lives like that, walking around on your city streets piled with debris from the bombs." Jack stood and sauntered to the living room window overlooking the terrace and woods. A smattering of old folks sat around red-covered patio tables, silver hair and bald heads bobbing in conversation. How many of them remember? How many scars remain?

He turned to Sherk. "Do you guess one more session tomorrow with Renate should finish the story?"

"Let's hope so," Sherk said.

Jack thought about going back to Chicago in another week. He was ready, even though he would miss Renate's hospitality, along with Sherk's family. And the biergartens, of course. Hard to beat the Hofbräuhaus. Still, he had no definite plans for his future. Just some vague ideas hovering around. Oh well, he'd land on his feet. Always did.

Half an hour later, Renate bustled into the room, chattering to Sherk. She seemed to have a second wind.

"We have over an hour until lunch time," Sherk told Jack. "Renate can tell more of the story now, and then wait for the rest tomorrow. That means another night in Weimar. Our hotel room is available until the weekend, so we're good."

Renate eased herself into her cushiony chair and waited until the men were comfortable.

Surprisingly, Jack wasn't bored from Renate's long dialogue in a foreign tongue. Instead, he found her sparrow-like body and facial expressions interesting as she talked, and he understood an occasional German word. In spite of her frail appearance, he guessed she was one tough apple strudel. Based on what Sherk had told him so far, she'd have to be.

CHAPTER 16
Renate – 1945

Thank you, Gentlemen, for allowing me to rest. Now, I'll go on.

Ariana made me promise never to tell a soul about what happened to her that day. But now I must.

·   ·   ·   ·   ·

Another hectic hour had passed in the hospital with no sign of Ariana. I was a wreck. Old men and women begged for medications to ease their pain, while children cried, some lying in their own waste. We tried to keep up, but with the shortage of doctors, nurses, and orderlies, it was hopeless. I grabbed Stefan's arm. *I'm going to hunt for Ariana. Something's happened to her. She should've been back two hours ago.*

I could tell he was worried too, otherwise he would've argued. *I'm coming with you, Renate. Let's go.*

A frazzled nurse wondered where we were going, but we rushed past her and hurried outside. The smoky odor almost gagged us, but something else too. A putrid, rotting stench I later learned came from dead bodies buried beneath slabs of concrete. Bombed-out apartment buildings stood like skeletons, their windows hollow eye sockets gazing at the ruins. How could this be happening to our beautiful city? And where was Ariana?

It was an unusually warm April day, but smog from the raids caused overcast skies. Distant sirens wailed as we ran down Parzivalstrasse beside the hospital, winding our way west. We turned onto the main street alongside Luitpold Park toward Opa's place. Ariana had said she'd take a short cut that I guessed would go north through an alley behind some shops and a school on the opposite side of the park.

We met several men riding bicycles, veering around piles of wreckage scattered on streets and sidewalks. A few gray-uniformed policemen wandered about looking as if they had a purpose, their black boots dingy. A young girl in a white blouse and plaid skirt strolled by walking her bicycle as if this were an ordinary day. I recall her white socks and brown shoes, loose laces trailing in their wake. Stefan warned her to find somewhere safe, but she didn't seem worried. Foolish girl. I remember hoping she wouldn't trip on her shoe laces.

We hurried down a narrow passageway around a corner, then back on the street. We almost reached the 2R highway when we heard a man yelling from our right. Stefan's hand darted out to stop me as we looked toward the voice.

Oh, Gott, I squinted to make out a policeman holding onto someone, stepping their way around overfilled trash bins behind a shuttered down café. My stomach told me it was Ariana.

From this point, my memory blurs into a watercolor of twilight and shadows. Voices, specters of people pop in my mind, and I can only tell what the officer, Ariana, and Stefan said. I must've run to Ariana and tried to hug her, the man telling me to let her go, she needed a doctor. Stefan's calm voice. *Take deep breaths, Renate. Look at me and breathe in and out slowly.* I can still feel his hands on my arms as he held me up.

I barely recall our stumbling back to the hospital with the policeman helping us, and bits of conversation from Ariana as she protested. *No, no, not the hospital. I'm not hurt. Can't let anyone see me. Don't tell. Gott, don't tell.* I wondered who she was pleading with. All of us I'm sure. But her arm was bloody and bent like a red toothpick. And what was she wearing? Not her white aproned uniform. The policeman held a man's brown, dirt-stained shirt around her shoulders, exposing her bare skin, her legs, no shoes, torn dirty stockings.

At the hospital, we gathered around, helping Ariana sit on an examining table. Someone pulled curtains around us for privacy, and all the time, she babbled on. *Can't you see? Not clean. You want to get Tripper?* It wasn't until hours later I understood.

We stayed overnight in hospital; I must've curled up on a chair. Memory fades. At one point Stefan made his way to Opa's home. He told them Ariana and I were so busy we were staying at work for a couple days. I didn't want our grandparents to wonder why we didn't come back that night.

Gradually, we found out what happened. Over the next three days, Ariana talked.

• • • • •

There were two of them, she said. They spotted her hurrying through an alleyway and called to her in broken German. She ran, and they started after her. The earlier warning pierced her brain. Escaped POW's. She was no match for them. Nowhere to hide. She stumbled over a chunk of concrete. Skinned her knee. Kept running.

Something crashed into her. On her knees. Screamed. Hit. Scratched. Kicked. Bit. Cloth ripping. Punching, slapping her face over and over. Obscenities. Fetid sweat. She smelled Jägermeister. Must've looted a liquor store.

Later, she told me this in private. *Oh, Renate, I had my monthly. They saw blood and got madder. Kicked. One on top of me. Then from a distance. Shouts.*

Halt! Geh weg. Gunfire. One. Two. Three. A ton of weight on me. Suffocating. Can't breathe. Can't breathe.

Her savior. A policeman named Alwin. His gray-green uniform loose on his body, tunic hanging over the black belt, his dusty boots. He'd been checking inside the café for looters when Ariana's screams pierced his ears. He'd raced outside and around to the back. Then he saw.

One man ran off and dodged the first bullet from Alwin's gun. The one on top of Ariana got two in the back. Alwin managed to shove the dead body off her, grunting, cursing. She sat up, holding her throat.

When he talked to us in the hospital, Alwin's anger was palpable. *The Scheisser's shirt and pants were off, so I used the shirt to cover her up. Her clothes –* He shook his head, looked down. At least he had the decency to appear uncomfortable.

Alwin had found an ID printed with a Polish name lying on the ground near the body. I still remember his face, red with rage when he told us. *Damn Scheisser, assaulting our women.* Pardon my language, but that's what he said.

After Ariana settled back in the hospital, he left us to return to his job. We never saw Alwin again. I have no idea what happened, but in the turmoil, I'm sure he returned to deal with the body. Or not.

•   •   •   •   •

How much time passed? Two days flowed into three, and by then, Ariana had almost healed physically. I was sure her arm was broken, but the doctor said he couldn't detect a fracture. She wore a sling for a couple days and kept the arm wrapped in a bandage.

Seeming in a daze much of the time, Ariana asked twice where Alwin was. She wanted to thank him again for saving her life. *I owe him so much, Renate. If he hadn't been there right then, I would've been – Mein Gott, I would have died – he was strangling me.* We had gotten wind of the rumors of the Red Army invading from the east, and what they did to women. I hated all men during those months.

Later, another day or so, Stefan said we needed to see our grandparents for their peace of mind. The next morning, he walked with us, helping Ariana along the way, until we reached their apartment.

Oma and Opa fussed over us, but they didn't seem to suspect Ariana had been attacked, since her sling and bandages were gone. When they noticed the bruises on her face and arms, she joked about her clumsiness, claiming she'd tripped over a bedpan, or a child at the hospital had clung onto her arms tight enough to cause bruising. She poked fun at herself, but Oma and Opa pressed their lips in a straight line.

Oma insisted we go to Mutti's house to check on her and Kurt. A train still ran once a day to Dachau, so Opa talked a neighbor into driving us to the Hauptbahnhof. When we arrived at the station, a throng of mainly women and children pushed and shoved, bedraggled in loose drab clothes, carrying battered suitcases. Policemen tried to maintain order. *Clear the way. No loitering. Check the schedules on the wall.*

Ariana and I plowed our way through and got in line to buy tickets, found the track to Dachau. We scrambled onto our car as we elbowed our way through the noisy, anxious crowd.

Twenty minutes later, the locomotive shrieked. Plumes of steam rolled over the track. As we chugged along toward Dachau, Ariana kept insisting that I promise not to tell Mutti what happened to her. *Renate, you can't tell Mutti. She'll have heart failure if she finds out.*

Don't' worry, I won't. I said that over and over.

But I'm afraid she'll guess by looking at me.

No, you look fine. The bruises barely show. I spoke the truth. Ariana was still a movie star, as lovely as ever, even though some cuts were visible on her neck and arms. Mute testimony of what she had endured.

• • • • •

In the days to come, Mutti either didn't notice the pale welts on Ariana's skin, or chose to remain silent. She was distraught over Kurt. He'd gone off with the Youth the week before, and he hadn't returned. She had retrieved her rosary beads from hibernation, and was praying over them throughout the days.

We stayed in the house with Frau Hilda, who would venture out each day to find food and listen to the news, mainly gossip about the expected end of the war. As you can imagine, things fell apart, the Allied armies marching toward Munich.

We managed to eat watery cabbage soup and light fires in the back yard for makeshift cooking. The explosions, the sirens blared constantly until we became numb to them. We moved like robots, just surviving. And there was Ariana.

I could tell she wasn't the same. Something had changed, shifted, like a lamp growing dim inside her, leaving darkness in its wake. As the days, months, and years passed, she'd tell me bits and pieces, but carefully portioned out for me listen to and sit in silence.

CHAPTER 17
Weimar

After the morning visit with Renate, Jack craved lunch and a pint. Sherk mentioned several restaurant options, but they ended up at the hotel bar. No annoying crowds or noise.

The day was warm but cloudy as they drove away from Renate's residential building. Young people rode bikes along the streets, dressed in black form-fitting sports clothes. Jack apparently was a dinosaur, and a poorly-dressed one at that. Was he the only person who still wore sweatpants?

Antsy to discover what Renate had said, Jack looked at Sherk. "Just tell me the gist of the conversation. I don't wanna wait till we eat."

Sherk seemed annoyed. "Jack, believe it or not, it's sometimes difficult to translate and try and remember everything Renate said. So, I need to step back and relax before I begin."

"Yeah, yeah. I'll try and relax myself." Fat chance of that.

Fifteen minutes later, they sat in the lounge of the Hotel Leonardo, unwinding on vinyl-cushioned bar stools, beers in hand.

Jack took a healthy swig of Warsteiner Dunkel, his recent brew of choice while in Germany. "Renate seemed drained this morning." He wiped his mouth with a napkin. "I'm finding her story interesting, but I wonder what it all has to do with Pa. I wonder when he'll come in."

"You need to be patient, Jack. Remember she said that you need to understand Ariana to get the full story with your dad. She should be fine after a day's break. Sherk straightened his wire-rimmed glasses. "This last conversation was a tough one. I'll update you up after we order."

"I get the idea you're stalling. Must've been something bad."

Sherk looked around the room. "Here comes a waiter. Just hold your horses, Jack."

The Leonardo was the opposite of a traditional European hotel. Its trendy, understated decor showcased red, orange, and black splashes of geometric prints on the walls, the design repeated on the carpets. Trim-looking men and women in dark business suits strode about, seemingly with great purpose.

A young red-haired bartender sidled over. "Have you decided?" His German accent not as pronounced as most, Jack noticed.

Sherk handed him their menus and ordered a burger for Jack, a bratwurst sampler plate for himself.

The redhead grinned, then hesitated, gazing at Jack. "Excuse me for staring, but you remind me of that American actor, ah—"

Jack gave half an eye-roll. "Yeah, nothing new. But he's Irish."

"Oh ya, right." he nodded. "Your food should be ready in ten, fifteen minutes." He turned and sauntered away.

Jack took another gulp of beer. "So what did I miss this morning?"

Sherk sighed. "Renate and Stefan, the medic at the hospital, decided to go hunt for Ariana since she'd been gone for several hours." He spoke for a few minutes, slowing down as he summarized the attack on Ariana.

Frowning, Jack said, "So these thugs were escaped POW's. One ran away, and the other got shot. And the cop came just in time, to stop Ariana from getting strangled."

"That's right. Renate said after a few days the details came out gradually, and Ariana told her she was having her period and—"

"Whoa, man, too much information." Jack was squeamish about women's bodily functions, even after years as a cop and his marriage. Karen used to tease about a tough guy like him being such a prude. God, how he still missed her after all these years.

Sherk shrugged. "Sorry, guess men your age don't want to give ear to the curse of Eve."

"Just drop it for chrissakes. All I need is at least Ariana came out alive." Even after his twenty-five-year experience as a cop, Jack's blood pressure still rose from conversations or witnessing the aftermath of sexual assault.

"Yeah, that was the important part, that she survived," Sherk agreed.

Sherk took another drink. "Well, after a few days, Renate and Ariana stayed at the grandparents' place not far from the hospital. Guess they were okay, but much of the city was in ruins. Her Opa wanted them to take the train to Dachau to check on their mother and Kurt, the brother."

"I thought he was off serving in the Hitler Youth."

"He was, but they hadn't gotten word about him for a while. That's where Renate stopped the story. They were on the train heading for their mother's place. Ariana was worried her mom would suspect that she'd been beaten up, and she made Renate promise never to tell."

Jack was so engrossed in the story, the bartender seemed to appear out of nowhere holding a tray of steaming sausages and a hamburger with German potato salad.

"Here you are, guys." He set the plates on the bar. "More beer for ya?"

"Jawohl," said Jack, impressed with his correct pronunciation, but still, the bartender gave him a patronizing smile. He took a bite from his thick, onion-laden burger. "Sehr gut." Again, impressed with himself. Anything to keep from dwelling on Ariana's ordeal.

"You'll be talking like a native soon, Jack." Sherk took his knife and fork, sawed off a hunk of bratwurst and bit into it. "I agree. The food's sehr gut."

Jack drained his mug and wiped his mouth. "That's the end of Renate's tale until tomorrow?"

"Yes, except she also said Ariana was never the same after that. Like a light diminished in her." Sherk shook his head and sighed. "Poor girl."

The bartender brought their beers and placed them beside the plates. "Anything else?"

"Nein," Jack told him.

"You're on a roll," Sherk said as carrot top wandered off.

"So tomorrow we should discover how Ariana and Pa met up. The part we've been waiting for." Jack took another bite of burger. "By the way, I emailed Tommy last night, hoping he'd tell me which regiment Pa was in. He'll check the discharge papers. I never thought about the specifics before. Just knew he was in the Army and was there for the liberation of Dachau."

Sherk set his fork down. "Yeah, I'm interested too. I did more research last night about the Seventh Army and which division actually was first to arrive at the camp. There's contradictory information on whether it was the forty-second Rainbow Division or the forth-fifth Thunderbirds."

"Can't see my old man in a division called Rainbows," Jack scoffed.

Sherk shook his head in mock annoyance. "Different connotation back then. Anyway, he probably was in the forty-second because the forty-fifth Division was Oklahoma-based. They didn't accept out- of-state recruits until right before the Korean War."

"Okay," Jack said. "But why the conflicting reports? Wouldn't the Army have documented who got to Dachau first?"

"Everything was bedlam." Sherk took a bite of potato salad. "The Americans were in shock when they found the camp. It was a week before the official end of the war, and both divisions wanted credit for the liberation. Look online and you'll see all the soldiers who wanted recognition for getting there first."

Jack rolled his eyes. "Gimme a break. Some pissing contest that was."

On second thought, wouldn't it be something if Cpl. John Bailey had been one of the first to witness the worst atrocities in history?

•   •   •   •   •

The next morning Jack and Sherk arrived at Renate's apartment at nine-thirty. Her sky-blue blouse matched her eyes, her cheeks flushed. After shooing them into the room, she offered the usual coffee and pastries. Because they'd just eaten breakfast at the hotel, Sherk declined.

Sitting on the sofa, Jack thought Renate seemed a little keyed up, but happy and excited. She eased herself into the armchair and reached for a worn-out folder or pamphlet and held it in her lap. Could be she had more pictures to show them. She looked at Jack, her eyes shimmering.

CHAPTER 18
Renate – 2012

Today I have a big surprise. This part of the story will be special to Jack because he'll understand the truth of what his father dealt with. That is why I have this notebook. Since we first met, I've been waiting for this day so I can show it to you.

You see, Ariana persuaded John to write down everything he witnessed when his Army unit came to Dachau. So he wrote this diary after the war in 1946. Yes, can you imagine it? Even though he said she wouldn't understand all the language, Ariana told him she wanted to learn more English in school. She promised she would learn his words, and some day she would return it to him.

When Ariana's memory started failing, she brought John's journal to me for safekeeping. *I want you to have this, Renate. When you pass, then it will go to Monika.*

I must've mentioned Ariana and her husband Walter had a daughter? Monika is her name. She has an excellent job and lives near Stuttgart. She was just here last week, and is good about visiting her Mutti, even though Ariana doesn't recognize her on most days.

But let's get back to John's journal. He didn't want to write the terrible details of what he witnessed, but she insisted he write them. For whatever reason, she needed the information. Perhaps for people to always remember?

So here it is for you to read. It begins in the winter of 1945, a few months before the war ended. That will lead up to how John met Ariana and the rest of their—I'm not sure what to call it, except what it was. Their love story.

Perhaps Jack would rather bring the notebook back to the hotel. Then he can take his time and read it by himself.

Chapter 19
Weimar

After Sherk translated Renate's words, Jack couldn't stop staring at the journal in her hand. His old man wrote a diary? Nothing frilly about it. Looked like a spiral notebook without the spirals, its brown leather cover worn to a shine, the corners frayed. He stood and turned to Sherk.

"Yeah, why don't we head for the hotel. Then I can concentrate on it." Jack shook his head. "God, this thing has been here for —"

"Sixty-six years," Sherk said. "If he wrote it in nineteen forty-six, then sixty-six years."

"Right, Einstein. Point is, it's pretty damn old."

Renate rose from her chair and handed the journal to Jack. His hands trembled as he slowly took it and held it cautiously, like a Fabergé egg. This notebook had belonged to his father, so light in Jack's hands, yet heavy on his heart. He turned to Sherk, his voice raspy. "Sure wasn't expecting this."

They walked toward the door, Renate chattering away.

Sherk turned to Jack. "She wants us to come back tomorrow to visit Ariana one more time."

"Fine with me." He guessed his father's journal would help him see Ariana in a different light.

They said their goodbyes to Renate and walked down the hallway.

Jack said, "We'll come back tomorrow to visit Ariana again, but I'm ready to ditch Weimar and head back to Munich."

"You don't say? We haven't toured the main palace or the Goethe garden house —"

"No offense, Sherk, but I like Chicago. Always been a big city guy except for those years in Texas. Damn near died of the heat. This town doesn't have the vibe of Munich, not to mention the biergartens."

•   •   •   •   •

Riding back to the hotel, Jack held the notebook in his lap and gazed out the window.

"Aren't you going to sneak a peek at it?" Sherk glanced over.

"Naw, I'll wait till I get to my room. You can amuse yourself while I dig into it. Go tour a palace or two." Jack wasn't sure what emotions the journal would evoke, but better they manifest themselves in private.

"Nah. No palaces for me today." Sherk stopped at a red light. "I'm going to lie down. Didn't sleep well last night. I was concerned about Erica and the tests she's having in a couple days."

Jack turned to him. "Shit, man, I forgot about that. I'm sure they'll be fine like last time." Easy for him to say.

Sherk sighed. "Yeah, she's been fatigued lately, but that's normal. We've been texting or talking every day, and she'll update me when she finds out something."

Jack was uneasy about Erica's well-being. The thought of Sherk's wife dying of ovarian cancer was something he tried not to worry about. He'd hate to see his old friend in the same boat as him. Losing Karen and his little Elizabeth had damn near killed him. He figured Sherk was anxious about Erica's illness and treatment, but did a good job of hiding it. He should broach the subject again, but surely Sherk was confident he could talk to Jack if he wanted. Guess women were better at communicating about personal stuff.

Still, he couldn't rid himself of his own selfishness. For days, Sherk had done nothing but help Jack chase after his own interests. He hoped his friend enjoyed the time spent, and didn't figure Jack was using him. He needed to dream up a way to repay his pal. But how?

•   •   •   •   •

Later in his room, Jack sat on the edge of the bed, staring at the journal in his lap. He ran his hand over its smooth, worn surface. Why was he hesitating? Did he truly want to get inside his old man's head? He might discover uncomfortable things about John Bailey's war record that he'd be better off repressing. He'd gotten word about some American soldiers breaking military laws. And there was the connection with Ariana. Didn't want to visualize his father getting it on with a woman other than Ma. Although, given the circumstances —

Jack told himself to quit being a chicken ass, so he slowly opened the cover. The first page was unlined, yellowed with thinning, creased edges. A faint musty smell drifted in the air. He recognized his father's large, steady handwriting, a tiny blob of ink hanging from the occasional stroke on a letter. Must've used a fountain pen. His gut tightening, Jack studied the words:

John Bailey, Cpl.
US Seventh Army 42nd Rainbow Division
June, 1946, Munich

He slowly turned the page.

CHAPTER 20
Journal Entry — June 3, 1946

Dear Ariana,

You wanted me to write everything I remember about the last couple years, but I won't include much military information. It would bore you. I'm skipping over a lot of our combat that happened far away from you and your family. After all, you didn't want a history book.

I'm sure you will go back to school or the university like you plan to do and learn enough English to read this. I hate to tell certain details, but you insisted. You said it will be important someday to you and my relatives as part of history. You might want to cross out the swear words, but remember, you said you wanted this notebook to be my true thoughts.

I'm no Hemingway and I'm like a fish out of water writing this, but here goes.

•　　•　　•　　•　　•

Winter, 1945

All of us in the squad were fed up and tired, ready for the damn war to end, just like everyone on the home front. In December of '44 we were in southern France for a short time, then headed north in kind of a zigzag pattern and ended up fighting along the German border in January of '45. It was freezing cold, water turned to ice in the bottoms of our foxholes.

Guys were sick. Coughing, fever and the runs. You don't want me to write what that was like, running to the makeshift latrines, buddies telling you to hurry up. Ariana, you don't appreshiate the value of decent toilet paper until you ain't got it.

Then in March, we crossed the Rhine and captured a few towns along the way, can't spell them though. We rode in trucks, jeeps, or armored vehicles, and even bicycles some guys snatched from deserted farms. It was still cold and snowy. Like we were in Siberia.

By mid-April, we seized nearby villages and suburbs of Nuremberg, and headed south. In late April we crossed the Danube at Donauwörth and made our way down toward Munich. Still colder than a~~witch's~~ than the Arctic, snowing off and on.

Our goal was to capture Munich, but we made an awful discovery along the way, just when we were nearing the outskirts. It was Sunday morning, April 29, and we were closing in on the city. We were freezing our asses off. The fields and trees, covered with snow. We wore those damn brown Ike jackets, as they were called, that weren't exactly parkas. Almost useless against the cold. I thought of those poor Red Army bastards coming from Russia.

Anyway, we noticed a string of railway cars on the tracks beside an empty-looking storage-type shed. They looked like abandoned boxcars, all shabby. It reminded me of a western movie, a cowboy riding up to a lonely scene, right in the middle of the boonies.

Since a lot of railroad tracks were bombed out, we thought we were just seeing another line of rail cars sitting there going nowhere. We got closer, a few guys jumped off the trucks and said they looked like cattle cars open on top. We got closer. I remember someone yelling.

"Hey, are those dead animals by the tracks?"

Then closer.

The men called out, 'Holy Fuck', over and over. The stench hit first. Rotting, putrid stink was like an attack on us. I pinched my nose and jumped from the tank and headed toward the tracks. Bullet holes riddled the sides of the wooden cars.

Then the discovery.

The corpses were human. Or had been.

Men swore, wept, vomited.

I was one of the first in my squad to look inside an open boxcar. I was hollering, "Don't look." Dumb on my part. Of course, they had to look.

In minutes, they all saw.

I tasted bile in my throat.

Oh God, Ariana. Piles of bones wrapped in skin were crammed inside the rail cars. Car after car, same cargo. Later we'd find out there were forty to sixty boxcars full of 4,800 prisoners.

Some corpses, eyes wide open, stared right at us, their liberators, too late to do them any good. I tried, but couldn't look away from them. They were like piles of bluish-gray mannequins. Ghastly remains of men, women, children. One little girl still had a pink ribbon tied around her hair. That choked me up. Someone must've cared about her.

Some bodies were naked, legs and arms two inches wide, hipbones jutting in the air. Others wore rags of gray striped cloth. Some fully clothed in prison uniforms. It struck us. These were no enemy prisoners of war. They were civilians. Women and children. They'd been starved, shot, or beaten to death.

Then there were the survivors. Some looked worse than the dead. One old woman's face was withered away like a rotting apple.

My buddy, Bill, pulled a groaning man from underneath the corpse of a woman, her hair like brown straw, dark circles carved under her eyes. The poor guy was whimpering in a foreign tongue, probably Polish, another buddy said. Bill carried him like a child onto a Jeep, his striped prison pants falling to his ankles. Poor man had no rear end at all.

I can't tell you how shocked and filled with rage we were. We craved revenge. Several men ran toward the railway shed trying to find the first SS guards they could. I remember they yelled, "Shoot those Nazi swine. Shoot the bastards."

But that would come later.

CHAPTER 21
Journal Entry

Ariana, I needed a break, so I put this away for a few hours. But now I'll write on.

The boxcars were crammed with bodies, like I wrote. Some had been crushed and suffocated, many starved to death. We found out later they had been stuck on the train for days without food or water. There were rumors of cannibalism but thank God I never saw any evidence.

We kept searching from car to car looking for survivors. Shit, what we witnessed, you should never have to see, Ariana. No one should. And all the while the stench. Human waste along with rotting corpses. One guy's head was bashed in, his brains oozing onto the ground by the tracks.

Me and Bill got to the 5th or 6th boxcar and looked inside. At first, it didn't dawn on me what the hell I saw. I asked Bill what it was.

Bill started to talk, then quit.

A bald skeleton of a man, head bent, sat moaning. I couldn't understand what we saw at first, but he sat beside two decaying bodies and another man who was barely alive. Bill asked the half-dead guy what happened to the man who kept groaning. Looked like he had some of his leg gone, lots of blood and seeping crud. Bill understood more German than me. Sein Bein wurde amputiert. Wundbrand.

Bill turned pale, gasped. His words are still in my head. 'Jesus, Bailey, his leg was amputated.' He guessed he had gangrene from frostbitten toes and feet. After everything I'd seen in combat, never saw anything like this. The guy kept wailing. The other man kept talking. Er hat es selbst abgeschnitten.

Bill covered his mouth and gagged. He translated that the guy somehow amputated his own leg. He had covered the stump with old paper he'd found somewhere. Clotted blood and brown, yellow pus turned the paper a greenish black color. Stunk like sewage.

I damn near gagged myself. I still can't get that sight out of my mind. We couldn't figure how the poor bastard got something sharp enough to cut off his own leg. Then somebody figured the gangrene had rotted away the skin and bone, so he just used his own hands.

We looked around, saw a few buddies. I hollered for help. Two guys came to the car. They damn near puked when we tried to lift the poor man up without hurting him more. He screamed like a banshee. I remember one of our GI's yelling that the leg was falling off. It was coming apart all over the soldier's arms as he tried to carry him. The paper was coming off the stump, looked like skin was crumbling, falling on the ground.

The rest was a blur. I may have blacked out. We finally got him in the truck. Someone said later the poor ~~son of a bitch~~ guy ended up in a makeshift hospital tent. Never found out if he survived. Just one of many I wondered about in months to come.

The Dachau Death Train, as it was later called, was the worst thing I'd ever seen. Until then the reasons for the war were pointless. I never realized why the hell we were fighting until now. Of course, we were in the war against the Germans, and we were invading their country on land, so they had to defend it, and we had to kill 'em.

But this whole war — way beyond battles over territory. I wasn't the only one who hated the Germans more than you can imagine. Seeing what they'd done. On this train.

At Dachau. Buchenwald. The others. Now fighting this war had a reason.

We were fighting evil. Actual evil. How could they do that to their own people?

What the hell was this? The middle ages?

This was in my lifetime, for God sake.

My own ~~fuckin'~~ lifetime.

CHAPTER 22
Weimar

Jack put the journal on the end table by his bed and wiped his brow. Why was he sweating? He couldn't wrap his head around his old man seeing all that. No wonder he took it out on his wife and kids after he came home. The drunken rages. The ruined Christmas dinners. No one could ever be the same after witnessing what he and his buddies saw. No way in hell could anyone even imagine what it was like. And there we were, in the decades that followed, lounging in our air-conditioned homes, complaining about lousy TV reception, putting on weight.

At the mini fridge, Jack opened a bottle of Pilsner and took a swig. But the images his father described assaulted his taste buds, and the beer almost came back up. His knees started to buckle so he steadied himself against the wall. Needed to sit back down. He was tempted to call Tommy or talk to Sherk about what he'd read. But his brother would have to wait until he was done with the whole thing, until he'd had a chance to absorb his father's words and hopefully become numb to the horror. Besides, he could hardly read it over the phone.

Just sit, Jack. Sit and breathe.

Hopefully Renate would give him the journal to keep. But wait— she'd said something about passing it on to Ariana's daughter. Damn, he'd forgotten about that. He'd get Sherk to talk to Renate. Since Jack's father wrote that journal, shouldn't it belong to him and Tommy?

He glanced at the notebook. Who was this soldier who wrote these words so many years ago? Jack couldn't separate his memories of his father at home in Chicago from the soldier trudging through frigid weather and coming upon those gruesome bodies. John Bailey must've been how old? Just a young guy. He was born in 1922, so he'd been around twenty-three. He also had a wife at home in Chicago. He and

Maureen O'Leary, Jack's mother, had married a year before he'd enlisted.

Jack thought of himself at that age. Drinking, carousing, community college between dead-end jobs. A carefree world then. He didn't get his shit together until his late twenties. Witnessing the horrors of Dachau, no wonder his old man was a mean drunk.

Jack glanced at the Pilsner bottle, but decided he had no taste for it. What had happened to him? The worn brown notebook rested on the table beside him. Like picking at an irresistible scab, he lifted the journal and found where he'd left off.

Swallowing hard and settling back against the pillows, his thoughts drifted back to April 29, 1945.

Chapter 23
Journal Entry — June 4, 1946

Ariana, I hope this hasn't been too much for you. Even now, a year after the war, most people in the States don't know what truly happened. When I wrote ma and pa just a few things about Dachau, they refused to swallow it.

About the death train. Some of the squads stayed around the tracks and helped survivors, others followed our sergeants into a large compound with a stone wall around it. We split up, some going on either side, where we met guys from another division. We made our way to a huge gate with "Arbeit Macht Frei" across the top of the iron entrance. I learned later those same words were on the gates of other camps. "Work Makes You Free." What bullshit.

Crowds of prisoners in gray stripes behind the gate were hollering, cheering, others silent, crying, moaning. We were their liberators. The Americans. The gate opened easy from the outside, the lieutenants and sergeants yelled at us to keep the prisoners inside.

A few German guards held back Rottweilers, barking and lunging, straining their leashes. The dogs acted crazy, as if they could tell something big was happening.

It took a while to get some kind of order. Our commander was Henning Linden, and he walked over near the gate and stood on top of one of the barriers over a narrow canal. He was shouting orders when a German lieutenant and a Red Cross worker with a white arm band approached, holding up truce flags. Our guys had their guns on them until Linden signaled the okay.

Lt. Heinrich Wicker (we learned his name later) carried surrender documents. He walked up to Linden and saluted with a "Heil Hitler," announcing he was ready to turn over the camp. So, Linden officially signed the Dachau surrender that afternoon of April 29.

After that, an American officer grabbed Wicker's arms, called him a "Schweinhund" and shoved him into a Jeep. They drove away and a couple minutes later, a gunshot cracked. That's what I was told later, but I didn't witness it.

I don't remember in what order things happened after that. Shouts of "Kill the bastards" could be heard over and over that day and the next few days too. Everything was madness. Even some of our boys walked around like they were shell shocked. I spoke to one guy, and he looked at me in a daze, said his mother was cooking pot roast for dinner. He probably ended up in a Section 8.

We saw piles and piles of clothing, and prisoners were hanging out upstairs windows of the stone jails. But others were walking outside by that time. Little kids called some of our guys "Papa" and hugged them. They hadn't seen their parents for so long, forgot what they looked like. One scrawny little boy wouldn't let go of a soldier's leg. He kept crying, "Papa" and some German words too. Poor kid. It was hard to watch.

In the midst of this, our sergeant told us to inspect the rest of the camp. We walked across the courtyard and crossed the canal that served as a makeshift moat. There we saw the gas chambers and crematoriums. Low brick buildings. Chimneys. Piles and piles of human ashes, some bones mixed in. The storage rooms were filled with grisly stacks of gassed prisoners.

A buddy later described the smell this way: When he was a kid, his mother would bring home a freshly killed chicken from the butcher. She'd hold it over the gas flame on the stove to burn the feathers off and some skin and fat would burn too. The stench was the same, except these were human bodies.

By then, we were ready to call it quits when this woman journalist who tagged along with our division came running over to us. Everyone thought she was a real pain in the ass, sticking her nose in everything and writing about it. She wasn't a bad looking broad, but she got in the way, like she was so fue frickin' important and smiling a lot.

Anyway, she was all excited and came running up to us, blabbing that Col. Felix Sparks of the 45th Infantry was walking through the residential part of the camp when he saw a Lt. Bill Walsh chasing a German soldier shouting: "You sons of bitches' over and over." So, Walsh caught the German and beat him on the head with the barrel of his rifle. Sparks yelled at him to stop, but Walsh kept beating the guy. He wouldn't stop, so Sparks cracked Walsh over the head with the butt of his .45. Walsh fell to the ground and laid there bawling like a baby.

After Sparks secured command, it took seven men to haul Walsh away. And while I'm on the subject, that Maggie Higgins journalist broad told us more the next day. She said after Walsh was hauled off, she followed Sparks' men to the coal yards where a group of 50 German prisoners were lined up in front of a wall. Sparks ordered that a machine gun be trained on them, but not to fire. Then a soldier called for Sparks, and he left. The machine gunner opened fire, then another GI shot his gun. Sparks ran back into the coal yard. He pulled out his .45 and fired into the air, yelling orders for his men to stop. But the machine gunner was still firing, so Sparks ran toward him and kicked him in the back. He dragged him away by the collar, away from the gun shouting, What the hell you doing? The soldier told Sparks the Germans were trying to get away, which I'm sure was a lie. Sparks saw about 17 Germans who had been killed. He ordered the injured to be taken to a hospital.

Ariana, I'm telling you this because you will catch wind of how American soldiers broke military law by shooting prisoners of war. Rumors flew around, and I'm not certain everything that the Higgins broad said was true. She worked for a New York newspaper, and I'm sure she was part of the group that brought charges against our boys for killing the Germans after the surrender of the camp. She said a photographer and cameraman had recorded what happened, and their reports and photos were sent to General Arthur White, the head of the Seventh Army.

I'm straying off the subject of the camp, but I want to tell you what happened after the killing of the SS guards. When the war ended, Sparks was ordered back to America. Before he left, they sent him to see General Patton, who had been made commander of Bavaria. Of course, Sparks was afraid he'd be court martialed for the killings of the Germans on his watch, but Patton dismissed all allegations against him. According to several buddies, Patton told Sparks the charges against him were a bunch of crap. He said these words to Sparks: "I'm going to tear up these goddamn papers on you and your men. You've been a damn fine soldier, now go home." I'll bet the story is true.

And now I'll get back to the next few days at the camp and write more about the death train.

CHAPTER 24
Journal Entry

Ariana, I couldn't get the death train out of my mind. Where did those 4,800 people come from? At first guys said they came from Buchenwald because the Allied troops were advancing, and they needed to get rid of the prisoners. The Germans were transporting them to Dachau to be gassed and cremated, but the camp ran out of coal, so they couldn't run the crematoriums. So, the inmates, dead and alive, were stuck in the train cars in freezing weather.

Later, I learned there were prisoners from other camps that met the Buchenwald train and were added on, so if that's true, that's why there were so many victims.

•   •   •   •   •

Back to the day after liberation, April 30. Part of our division was ordered to soldier on to Munich, but my platoon stayed at the camp to help with sick prisoners. I admit I was relieved. I don't want to sound yellow, but no one was certain what lay in wait for our guys in the city. Besides, if I'd gone to Munich, I never would have met you, Ariana. Maybe there is such a thing as fate.

The 7th Army took over, and by then they said there were over 30,000 prisoners at the camp. I wondered if it was true. The next day a group of Army doctors and other military personnel formed a displaced persons and hospital team. They came with truckloads of food and medical supplies. A couple days later, two more evacuation hospitals came and set up in empty prisoner barracks that we'd cleaned out. We scrubbed them out to make billets for our living quarters. It was a godawful job, we threw out filthy, bloody, shabby blankets, swept up rat droppings all over the floors, used bleach to try and sanitize everything.

By now you know about the typhus epidemic, not unusual during war, spreading in camps and to the soldiers too. The disease killed about 400 prisoners a day. The Army contributed enough DDT powder for dusting the inmates to kill the lice that cause the spread to other people. After we bathed and dusted them with DDT, the prisoners were given clean pajamas, and their old prison clothes were burned. I did the same jobs you and Renate had when you were Red Cross nurse's aides at the Munich hospital. I made up beds that were lined up along opposite walls, with no curtains between them for privacy. We stocked medications, bandages, syringes. I carried my share of bedpans. The place stunk like a sewer most of the time.

The official typhus quarantine also called for the dusting of Army personnel, visitors, etc. We had to show our immunization records and were given the typhus shots unless we had gotten them in the last thirty days. They wanted to inoculate all the prisoners, but there wasn't enough vaccine on hand.

It was shocking how scared the sick prisoners were of us, even when we tried to give them vitamin shots. After how they'd been treated by the Nazis, they didn't trust anyone, except a few of them clung to some nurses like they were their mothers.

Then came the day we had long waited for—May 7. Word spread that Germany was about to at long last surrender to the Allies. As the day passed along, our sergeant said that General Jodl traveled to Reims and signed the unconditional surrender of the German forces. Everyone shouted, cried, and even without understanding English, the prisoners understood what happened. The next day was declared VE Day.

You wondered how I felt, but it's hard to put into words. Naturally, I was relieved and happy and confused all at once. We still had jobs to do at the camp, and I didn't get what the future would hold for me and my buddies. Our officers reported that some divisions would stay on for the occupation, but at first no one was sure if or how Germany would be divided among the Allied countries.

It took a while for the U.S., Britain, and the Soviets to negotiate the terms for the end of the war. But that summer at Potsdam, they signed the declaration, and the Americans got Bavaria and other parts of Germany as well. Of course, that was good news to me since that included Munich. I did not want to be far away from you.

Ariana, I wanted to tell you how American troops first marched into the town (Dachau), and saw this pretty little village, and were mad as hell that it was right next to the horrors of the camp. I was real angry when I learned about it too. Just the idea that regular people lived next door to all that suffering caused by their own people.

The following week, the U.S. Army commandant of the town (can't recall his name) after the liberation, brought about 30 high-ranking Dachau citizens to witness the camp. He was furious. He told them that their town should be sacked and turned into ashes.

The local priest was among the visitors, and they swore he got down on his knees and begged the Americans not to destroy the town. He may have saved it, but I'm sure he wasn't blind to what was happening in the camp. According to rumors, the Vatican and the Reich were in cahoots, from the concordat back when Hitler came to power. I won't go into all that, but Ariana, even as a not so faithful Catholic, I reckon the Church turned a blind eye to what was happening.

A day or so later, our staff sergeant told us our squad was joining the platoon assigned to go into the town and force more citizens to visit the camp and see for themselves what their country had done. It was a damn good idea. Let them see what their great Führer had done.

I was happy to get out of hospital duty. I didn't mind helping, but it was taking longer to rid the place of typhus than we thought, and I was getting sick and tired of blood and bedpans. Those nurses all deserved medals. For sure, so do you, Ariana, and your sister.

After we got our orders and assignments, we formed groups of three to go knocking on doors in the village. It was a warm, bright day, and things were peaceful in town, but people were hiding in their houses because they were scared, even though the war was over. Some men and women had to be almost dragged outside to wait until we got a certain number in our group. I was glad to see the bastards cowering in their homes. I wanted to stick their noses right in the decaying corpses. I am sorry for that now, because most of them, like you and your family were innocent people.

Ariana, I will always remember that sunny day we came to a house, small and gray with white trim. We walked up to the porch, and the lilacs were out. My ma had lilacs in Chicago, so I saw them before. I remember they smelled like perfume.

No one answered our knocks, so we banged on the door, and I can still recall us hollering. "Come out right now, or we're coming in." The door cracked open, and a gray-haired woman peered at us. We stepped inside and went through our drill, shouting for everyone in the house to come forward.

It was hard with the language, but I was lucky to have Bill along to help translate. He found out the woman's name, it was Hilda. She didn't seem afraid of us, talking so fast, Bill barely comprehended, but he figured that more people were in a bedroom down the hall because she kept glancing in that direction. Hilda kept trying to stop us from heading that way, and she grabbed my arm, then looked at me, and with a startled look on her face, suddenly jerked her hand away, as if it dawned on her I was the one in command.

Bill knocked on the bedroom door and forced it open. Two women huddled together on the bed, one older, one young. Bill tried to tell them they needed to come with us, and they were not going to be hurt. Then he said there might be more people, so we looked around. I opened the closet door, and through the dim light I saw a bunch of hanging dresses and blouses pushed to one side and a pile of clothes underneath.

I was aware of the women trying to stop me, but I leaned in and shoved the dresses away. A white shoe peeked out from the pile on the floor. I slowly pulled back the garment covering most of the shoe, and then saw a pair of legs, knees bent. A muffled cry came out, and I peeled off the rest of the covering. Looking up at me through sky blue eyes, was the most beautiful girl I'd ever seen.

CHAPTER 25
Weimar

Jack's stomach tightened as he read the last words. His old man calling another woman the most beautiful girl? Even though Jack hadn't been born then, anger and a sense of betrayal coursed through his veins. He harbored a protective loyalty to his mother back in Chicago waiting for her husband to return from the war. She'd be devastated, even today, if she found out.

A knock on the door interrupted his thoughts. He put the journal on the nightstand beside the untouched beer bottle, took a deep breath, and headed for the door, figuring it was Sherk. Who else would it be?

"How's the journal coming along?" Sherk wandered in and sat in the red vinyl armchair beside the TV.

"Depressing, tragic in parts. I had to take a couple breaks." An understatement, for sure.

"Yeah, I can imagine." Sherk started to speak, but stopped. His fingers anxiously scratched at the red vinyl. He turned to Jack. "Anyway, I just talked to Erica. She's doing well, she claims. I can't help but worry, though." Jack thought he noticed a catch in Sherk's voice.

Jack sat on the bed. "Yeah, I guess you would. Glad she's better." Sounded like a broken record, but one of these days, he'd encourage Sherk to talk more about his wife. For now, his thoughts were elsewhere. "Want a Pilsner?"

"A little early to imbibe, but why not?"

"Just opened one myself," Jack lied. He picked up his neglected bottle and took a measured sip, room temperature now, but he didn't let his distaste show.

He strolled to the mini-bar. Handed a bottle to Sherk.

Sherk raised the bottle. *"Ho! Ho! Ho! To the bottle I go/ To heal my heart and drown my woe..."*

The scene struck Jack as pathetic, two grown men, with other things on their minds, engaging in a façade of beer-guzzling frat boy mentality. Still, he played along.

"Finally, one of your Shakespeare quotes I can understand." Jack took a swig.

"J.R.R. Tolkien."

"Okay. Not a fan of that sci-fi crap."

"Actually, it's fantasy, and some critics thought one part was an allegory for the atomic bomb, but the themes are open to—"

"I'd love to listen to your dissertation, but I have more interesting things on my mind, no offense to J.R.R." Jack nodded at the journal.

"I'll take that as a subtle hint I should depart." Sherk started to rise.

"I won't take much longer to finish," Jack said. "Then I want you to read it. I'll have stuff to talk over afterwards." Jack set his beer on the table. "By the way, do you reckon Renate would let me keep the journal, since I'm John's son? I get she wants Ariana's daughter to have it, but who would've dreamed I'd show up?"

Sherk paused. "I'll need to word it very carefully and see how serious Renate considers her agreement with Ariana. It's like a death bed promise, except Ariana's alive, even though she wouldn't be the wiser." He straightened his glasses. "I'm not sure her daughter knows about the affair, and possibly she'd be better off if it is a secret. Germans are tight-lipped about personal things like that."

"Okay, we'll figure something out. See ya in an hour or two." Sherk started for the door, carrying his beer.

"Sherk."

Sherk turned.

"Erica will be fine. She's a strong woman."

Sherk gave a weak nod. Then he tipped his beer to Jack and let the door click as it closed behind him.

Jack settled back with the journal and turned the pages until he found the beautiful girl hiding in a closet.

CHAPTER 26
Journal Entry — June 5, 1946

Ariana, when I saw you in that closet, I froze. I didn't move for a couple seconds, but it seemed longer. God, you were a living doll, Ariana. You reminded me of an American movie star. And you were so scared, scared of me. I wanted to take you in my arms where you'd be safe. This ~~don't~~ doesn't sound like me. I thought I was tougher than that.

You've lost some memory about those few days, but I recall helping you up and out of the closet. You whimpered, and I saw faded purple bruises on your arms. You didn't say anything at first, your eyes kept darting between me and my buddies. We stood in the bedroom, Bill telling you not to be afraid. You and your mother and sister clearly were scared and didn't like us, but Hilda stood her ground, jabbering on like she had something important to tell us.

Then she offered us coffee. We were surprised, but we looked at each other and shrugged. Fraternizing with the enemy was against the rules, but what the hell, we didn't give a damn about anything then, and I couldn't remember the last time I'd had a decent cup of coffee.

We sat at the kitchen table. Your mother tried to help Hilda with serving us, and dropped a saucer, so Hilda shooed her away. You and your sister just stood around acting nervous. You kept looking at me, and I couldn't keep my eyes off you. There we sat, drinking coffee and eating cherry strudel like we were visiting our grandmothers back home.

Hilda seemed to know why we were there, that we wanted people to come with us and witness the camp. Bill finally got her to stop talking so fast. We learned that you and Renate had been Red Cross nurses in Munich, and your brother Fritz had been sent to Switzerland. Hilda begged us not to make you ladies go see the camp.

My two buddies and I debated about it, we decided to give you a pass. But the real reason we looked the other way was what Hilda said: a few months after Kristallnacht, your papa had been thrown in Dachau prison for being a Social Democrat. Then we realized you were good people, brave people who had tried to resist the Nazis. That was when I started to understand.

We agreed that if anyone was curious, we'd claim you were all sick with what might be typhus. Hilda told us you all would pretend to be ill and not come outside for a week, in case their neighbors got suspicious.

By this time other guys from the squad had taken groups of citizens away, and there were about ten people waiting in the street. I didn't want to leave you, Ariana, so I took you aside. I'll come back and see you tonight. I remember speaking those words, and you looked at me as if you understood what I said. I didn't get at the time that you understood a little English. I was determined to see you again, not only because you were beautiful, but I sensed there was something inside of you that I wanted to find—oh, I can't explain this very well, but you said later that you were attracted to me right away too.

The day dragged on. Ariana, I was so relieved that you weren't with us to witness the camp. Even children were forced to look at the piles of bodies, and a few days later, members of the Hitler Youth were brought in to see exactly what they'd been fighting for. I bet your brother Kurt got an eyeful.

A week later when he turned up at your house, he denied seeing the camp, but you and I didn't fall for it. He clammed up and wouldn't talk about his involvement in the Youth the last years of the war. He didn't want to upset your Mutti. Remember how she wouldn't quit hugging him?

You realized later how the townspeople reacted to the sights at the camp. Some got sick, almost everyone turned their heads away, some kept muttering they had no idea what had gone on. Even though I didn't understand much German, I could tell what they meant. Most of them acted shocked.

Since you and your family didn't have to help bury the bodies, I will write about it because you wanted me to. Over two weeks after the Dachau liberation, burial of the dead began. By then a lot of the bodies were falling apart because they were rotting. You see, they had been left out in the open on purpose to show as many townsfolk and U.S. soldiers as they could, and also to take photographs, to have proof for all the world to see.

I hate to write this, but the Americans forced some women citizens of Dachau to disinfect the boxcars of the death train. None of them were given any protection against typhus, no rubber gloves to handle the corpses. You can imagine what they had to put up with because of the decomposing bodies.

The US Army demanded that the farmers parade their open wagons of bodies, circling through the town for the citizens to see again. Then they had to haul the dead inmates to a hill north of the camp and bury them in mass graves. I found out later that the corpses were added to bodies already buried in the graves from before, when the camp ran out of coal for the crematoriums. A buddy said he was struck at how the woods around the hill looked so green and pretty and peaceful. That's what they call ironic.

About what happened with the camp afterwards, besides giving medical care for the prisoners, it was used as a prison for German soldiers and also a displaced person center. It housed mostly eastern German refugees who were driven from their homes.

I also need to write about your Papa because you wanted me to. After you told me his full name plus the month and year he was imprisoned, I took some time off and checked at the Administration offices, where a couple guys helped me go through files until we found him listed. I remember the night me and Bill told you and Renate that your Papa died of typhus in November of 1944. We hated to tell you, but you begged us for information as to what happened to his body. Truth was, he may have been buried in the mass grave at Leitenberg Hill, since they ran out of coal around that time. Many political prisoners before him were cremated and the ashes were sent to the families. Maybe I shouldn't write that, but at least your papa lived longer than a lot of others.

You and Renate broke the news to your Mutti later. You said she wailed and carried on like she was crazy. At the end, you got her to settle down, and be grateful that at least the rest of the Schröders survived. Fritz was alive and would come home from Switzerland later in June, and Kurt had shown up thin, but unharmed. I want to write that Fritz was happy, and you thought he was treated in a good way at the place he was sent to. I liked it when you and me took him to the park for a picnic one time and a few times we played Sternhalma with him.

It was like Chinese checkers and he was good at it and even sat still for a few minutes. Then he would get up and pace around. Anyway, he was always a good person.

·   ·   ·   ·   ·

Ariana, I'm coming to the end of this, and I don't want to write about you and me together because it is our own private business. But I have some thoughts I want you to never forget.

You and your parents and Renate are the opposite of people's opinion of the Germans. A lot of people would blame you just for being born into a German family. The world will despise your country and its people for a long time, even though it's unfair. Innocent people like you didn't cause the war. But I guess that's human nature, to blame a whole country.

People say war makes a man out of you. In some ways, that's true for me. Sometimes I feel like an old man who has seen the worst of people.

But my buddy, Bill has said more than once, that he saw good people do bad things and bad people do good things. He's a smart guy. He was in college in Oklahoma when he dropped out to enlist. He told me one important thing he will tell his children and grandchildren: he saw the strong become weak and the weak become strong. I should have found out exactly what he meant.

So now we both wait for my orders. I may soon be discharged and shipped home like some guys in our division. I don't want to leave, but family and duty wait for me in America. I can't come up with words to describe this whole life with you, so I will close for now.

Ariana, I will always remember you no matter what happens. I am a better man because of you.

I'll see you in every lovely summer's day,

Love,

John

P.S. I signed off with a line from our special song because as you know, I could never dream up words like that.

CHAPTER 27
Weimar

Jack read the last page, his mood sinking. Why did he have a sense of disappointment after finishing his father's story? He hadn't been this mystified since he found the damn letter a few months ago in the cardboard box.

He stood and stretched. The rumble in his stomach indicated he needed to eat, but he was too distracted to obsess over food. Walking to the window, he thought about his father as a young soldier, away from home, and the horrific effects of war on the innocent, not to mention destruction of land, buildings, homes. No doubt about it. War was hell.

After gazing at the green lawn and landscaped purple flowers, Jack returned to the bed. He picked up the journal and read the first page again. "June 5,1946," he said aloud. Sixty-six years ago. Since the journal stopped before John Bailey was shipped home, Jack would remind Tommy to check the discharge papers for the exact date.

He still didn't perceive much about his father's relationship with Ariana, but their love was undeniable. In the journal, his dad described lots of terrible things he'd witnessed the last few months of the war, allowing Jack more insight into John Bailey's character. More than that, though. Words escaped him, yet the whole experience and knowledge he'd gained was something beyond the norm. Something superior. Other-worldly. A new way of viewing life.

He reached for another beer in the mini-bar, opened the cap, and took a drink.

But how far did things go with Ariana? From the letter she'd written years ago, it sounded like they were hot and heavy. Also, his father wrote that he had duties at home, which indicated he resisted, or at least tried to resist, the temptation of forbidden love. Though he'd been a lapsed Catholic, still you always have some level of guilt taking up residence in your bones.

Mulling over these questions, Jack aimlessly leafed through the rest of the blank pages of the journal. He almost reached the end when he stopped and stared at a page filled with handwritten German words. He recognized the handwriting from Ariana's long-ago letter. He turned several more pages and came to the end.

Rubbing the sandpaper stubble of his beard, Jack looked hard at the signature. He couldn't tell what the word was, but the first letter looked like a *D* followed by an *L.*

He punched in Sherk's room number on the phone. "Come on over. Just walk in, the door's unlocked."

Several seconds later, Sherk stepped in. "What's up? Ready for an early dinner?"

"Yeah, but I want you to translate this first." Jack held out the journal. "Start here."

Sherk sat in the armchair and took the notebook, looking at the page Jack held open with his thumb. "Hmm. Looks like Ariana added a postscript in your dad's journal."

"Can't get much past you, Sherlock." Jack plopped down on the bed. "What does it say?"

"Give me a minute." After reading silently, Sherk looked up. "A little personal in some parts, Jack. You sure you want to tune in to all this?"

"How personal? Like graphic stuff?"

Sherk cleared his throat. "No, not descriptive, except some intense emotions about their—ah—relationship."

Jack thought a moment. Did he want to dig into this? None of his business, but then, his old man was in his grave and Ariana's mind wasn't in the real world anyway. "I'm not sure, but I figure by now I've read about the war shit he saw, I should discover this too."

Jack gazed at the window. Ghastly terrors his father described had fostered a previously-missing respect for the man. How could you not respect someone who had seen the things he'd seen, and then be forced to live with ceaseless nightmares for decades? But this—affection or whatever his father shared with another woman—this could change all that.

Chest pounding, he looked at Sherk, and words, like caution cast to the wind, escaped him. "Go ahead. Spit it out."

He took a deep breath. "I'll grab you a beer to help things along." He retrieved another Pilsner from the mini-bar, popped the cap, and handed Sherk the bottle.

Sherk took a long drink. "The message will lose something in translation, but I'll do what I can. Here goes."

Jack willed himself to relax. If things got too sappy, he'd tell Sherk to stop. He took a gulp of beer and listened to a woman's long-ago words.

"June 24, 1946," Sherk began.

"Dearest John,

I am writing at the end of your diary because I want to always remember our time together. I will keep this in a safe place, and no one will see it except me.

I have been so heartbroken since you left for America a week ago. Ah, how hard it is to understand my emotions and yours too. If only you were free. Then we could live our lives somewhere, I wouldn't care where. Just as long as you were with me.

But we know you must stay with your wife, until the day might come for us to meet again. Your words of love will always be in my soul. I will cherish my time with you, especially when our love reached the most beautiful moments in the world these past few months. My whole being aches for you every night.

My heart is breaking, darling. I have never had such sorrow. I will always remember the special things, like finding the little Gasthaus in town where we snuck out at night to meet. We sat there drinking wine or beer at our little table by the back window as we held hands and listened to the song about always seeing each other when we looked at the moon. Bing Crosby sang it on the radio. You said the song was written just for us.

I was so happy when you and Bill got transferred to Munich last fall and we could have more time together because by then I was working at the hospital again with Renate. After a few months we didn't hide our courtship, since other American soldiers were seeing German girls. You said the officials gave up on the no-fraternizing rule, and we were so much in love, we didn't care.

You said my eyes were the color of the sky, and my skin was like peaches and cream. I remember I said, "Oh, John. That sounds so beautiful." And you said, "Well, that's what you are." You were so tall and strong and handsome. I noticed your sharp blue eyes right away. I remember how afraid I was at first in the closet, but the way you looked at me, I was sure I was safe.

Ah, the memories we made. You sang the song about sitting under the apple tree to me. You said you were off-key, but I loved your deep voice. You tried to tell me what the songs meant, like our song about seeing each other even when we were apart. It was so romantic and sad. You said, "I'm no Bing Crosby, but here goes." Then you'd sing, and I would get tears in my eyes.

You started to speak more German words, and I quickly learned many English words. I will go back to University and study more.

This diary will forever be with me, hidden where no one can see. And in the back, I am placing the picture Bill took of you and me by the river where we were on a picnic one day when it wasn't raining. It will be safe within these pages to be cherished forever."

•   •   •   •   •

Jack leaned forward "Oh, let's see the picture."

Sherk looked up. "Jack, you're spoiling the message here. It's almost finished. Just wait."

Jack rolled his eyes. "Sorry."

•   •   •   •   •

Sherk continued the translation. "I hope and pray that someday we meet again, even though I could tell you did not think so. You said the war damaged part of you, but I said not the most important part. I hope you will be happy, and not worry about me, but I will never be the same either. Losing my Papa, afraid the bombs would kill us, people hungry and sick, and myself being damaged a short time before I met you.

I am going to end this letter to you my love, with the words to another song we loved because we were happy, even when it rained so much that summer.

Through my tears, I write these lines.

So keep on looking for a bluebird

And list'ning for his song

Whenever April showers come along

John, my darling, may we always see a bluebird.

My love, always and forever,

Your Sweetheart"

CHAPTER 28
Weimar

A lump arose in Jack's throat. Was he getting soft? Possibly Ariana's last words triggered a memory of Karen. Then it struck him. The word. Bluebird.

"My God, Sherk, she wrote 'bluebird.'"

"Yeah, it hit me too. That's what Ariana was speaking when she last saw you. Now it makes sense. And her bird pictures. The sound of your voice and perhaps your eyes sparked that memory."

Jack shook his head. "Man, how unreal is that? How the brain works."

"Yes, and I wonder if anyone will ever explain it." Sherk looked at the journal, turned the page and then another. He hesitated before carefully removing a small, black-and-white photo, faintly yellowed around the edges. "Here, Jack."

"Oh, great. The picture. Thanks." Jack took the photo as if it were contaminated. He looked closely and saw a young couple, happy, arms around each other standing beside a tree. He turned the snapshot over and read aloud the words written on the back: "Ari und John, May 30, 1946."

He turned the picture back and gazed at the young woman, her blond hair swept up on her forehead, waves behind her ears falling to her shoulders. She wore a polka dot short-sleeved dress tied with a ribbon around her waist, its tails streaming down the front. The soldier, in a long-sleeved Army shirt, a cigarette dangling between his fingers.

Jack held the photo out so Sherk could see. "That's Pa all right. Must be a Chesterfield he's holding. He smoked them till the day he died of lung cancer."

"Seems like everyone smoked back then." Sherk shook his head. "Yes, times have changed."

Jack nodded. "Actually, it's still hard to see the guy I recall from childhood as this happy soldier with a beautiful girl."

"We all react that way about visualizing our parents as young people. Look at Ariana. She was quite the beauty. True, she does resemble Ms. Bergman."

Jack studied the smiling face. "Here's lookin' at you, kid,"

"Not bad, Bogie." Sherk placed the journal on the end table. "You've certainly learned more about your dad than most people ever register about their parents. I'm certainly well acquainted with John and Ariana too."

"Yeah, I'm gonna give you the journal to read tonight, so you can get the whole story. I mean, that is, if you want to."

"Sure thing. I'd like to read it if it isn't too personal." Sherk picked up the notebook.

"Hell." Jack shrugged. "You just read the most personal part." He looked Sherk in the eye with both a pang of guilt and the warmth of gratitude. "I'd appreciate you reading it. It's gritty in places, but you're already aware of a lot of it, like the atrocities in the camps."

Jack tucked the photo in his shirt pocket. "I'm muddled about the whole thing, mainly about Ariana. I'm not sure I'm better off knowing that stuff."

"Ignorance can be bliss, huh?" Sherk nodded. "It'll take awhile to process. You've had lots of emotional information to absorb these last few days."

"You sound like a shrink. I'll need one after this." Jack recalled his psychiatrists in Chicago and Texas when he needed help coping with his family trauma. He still walked around with the nuclear fallout of losing his wife and daughter in the car bombing all those years ago. Would he ever be able to put Karen to rest in order to find love, or at least companionship? Highly doubtful.

"I've always thought you could benefit from counseling, Jack."

"Yeah, that's a familiar song." He stood and wiped his hand across his mouth. "Actually, I'm beat. Tired of all this. Tired of concentrating on it. I need food and a Jameson, not necessarily in that order."

"Okay with me," Sherk agreed. "It would do us good to get out in the fresh air and into a pub."

Jack was relieved. Yes, it would be good to get out, out of the stuffy hotel room which unleashed family skeletons, forbidden photographs, and grown-ass men wallowing in too much booze.

• • • • •

Strolling down Belvedere Allee alongside the peaceful green park helped boost Jack's mood. The air was cool, and the sun peeked from behind clouds draped across calm late afternoon skies.

After walking in silence for several minutes, Jack spotted a small restaurant called The Lion across the street surrounded by verdant bushes and trees.

"How 'bout that place? Not many cars there. Hopefully not crowded," Jack said.

Sherk stopped and looked. "I agree. And I don't need to tell you, *Unquiet meals make ill digestions.*"

"I suppose you're gonna tell me that's not our pal Shakespeare."

"Actually, it is, from Richard the Third, as he's arriving —"

"Let's go. Coast's clear." Jack took advantage of a convenient lapse in traffic, stepped off the curb, and headed across the street, Sherk close behind.

"Sorry to interrupt the King Richard lecture," Jack called over his shoulder. "You can finish later."

"Sure, Jack. I'll try again after you imbibe a little palatable Bavarian whisky."

They walked past a small parking lot to the entrance of The Lion, a light stone tavern with black trim, a golden bronze image of a lion above the door, keeping fierce vigil over the patrons entering through the portals.

The interior was dark, with understated décor. Wood paneled walls were bare, except a large poster hung beside the bar, proudly displaying a coat of arms, its menacing golden lions holding onto the iconic crest. A young couple with two small children, one in a highchair, sat at a table by the window. Jack glanced around, hoping to sit away from the yammering kids.

"Over here," he said, pointing to a booth in a far corner. "We lucked out. Last thing I want to put up with are brats yakking, even though it's less annoying when it's in German."

They slid into brown cushioned seats. Jack barely noticed the other diners, so with luck he'd eat and drink in peace. A man with wild, Einstein-like hair, his face mapped with wrinkles, appeared and handed them menus. Pouches under his eyes seemed to weigh down the corners of his mouth.

"Schön etwas zu trinken?"

Sherk ordered an Augustiner, checked with Jack, and ordered him a Slyrs and a glass of water. It didn't hold a candle to Jameson, but you can't have everything. He'd order a beer chaser with the next shot.

"I'll bet that guy was in the war," Jack said, indicating the waiter.

Sherk shrugged. "He may not be old enough to have fought in the war, yet no doubt can remember it. He seems to carry sorrow around like a yoke."

Jack studied the menu. "Order me something that resembles a burger, or bratwurst would be okay."

"Will do." Sherk thumbed through the selections. "You ready to discuss seeing Renate tomorrow?"

Jack paused. "Yeah, the main thing is whether I can keep the journal. I hope she agrees to hand it over, but if not, I could make a copy. Wouldn't be the same though." The scent of smoked sausage drifted through the area as a young woman walked past with someone else's steaming dinner. Jack's mouth watered.

"I'm sure Renate would agree to a copy, but she may want to keep the last few pages that Ariana wrote." Sherk pushed his corn-colored hair from his forehead.

"Sure, no problem, her daughter may want to read it. It's not X-rated, more like a Hallmark card."

"Yeah, though remember, Jack, Ariana was only about nineteen or twenty when she wrote that." Sherk removed his glasses and cleaned them with a cloth. "You remember young love."

"Like it was yesterday."

Sherk scoffed. "Her daughter may not know about their affair, so the journal may be off-limits until Ariana dies."

The waiter brought their drinks, and Sherk ordered dinner.

Jack knocked back his whisky. "Time flies. Three more days till we head for Chicago. No offense to your native land, but I'm ready to go home."

"Yes, I'll be relieved to get back to Erica and the kids. I hope she's doing as well as she claims." Sherk's chin twitched.

"Yeah, me too. Any news about the tests she had?"

"No, but I'm expecting her to call tonight." Sherk took a drink from his beer mug.

Reluctant to push the conversation, Jack hoped Erica would beat the cancer. He didn't want to compare Sherk's situation with the deaths of his wife and daughter. Not right then anyway.

Suddenly, a piercing shriek filled the air, turning their heads toward the family across the room. The kid in the highchair kept screaming and flailing his arms, his mother standing, ready to lift him up.

"Jeez, sounds like a wounded hyena, and he ain't laughing," Jack said.

Sherk shrugged his shoulders. "Yes, so much for Richard the Third's unquiet meal."

The kid bayed at an imaginary moon, and eventually shut up when the mother put him on her lap and stuffed something in his mouth.

"Thank God," Jack said. "About the journal, I'll be curious how Tommy will react, since the old man took his anger out on him the worst. I'm unsure about letting the other kids read it. But then, they should have a right to see their pa's war side, even though they'll find out about the affair with Ariana."

"It's always debatable what people have the right to know, above all in a family like yours." Sherk frowned. "Since your other brothers and sister are adults, they'll be able to handle the truth. But on the other hand, will the truth benefit them or hurt them? With your mum, she's better off with the secret."

"Right. Tommy didn't want to tell her about the letter either. She may be interested in some of Pa's war stuff he wrote about, but he writes Ariana's name off and on, so that wouldn't work."

Sherk rubbed his chin. *"Ah, yes. The pure and simple truth is rarely pure and never simple."*

"Couldn't agree more with the Bard on that one."

"Oscar Wilde."

"Figures." Jack took a gulp of water. "Anyway, I'm ready for another shot with a beer chaser. You wanna go see the barkeep, since he wouldn't understand me." Again, his lack of German language skills had served its purpose.

•   •   •   •   •

After finishing their food and drink, Jack offered to pay the tab. The thought of returning to Chicago with the journal gave him a lift, and

Sherk deserved a medal for tolerating his shenanigans, another of his mother's expressions.

They flung open the front door of The Lion and aimed themselves toward the hotel.

"Look at that, Jack." Sherk pointed to the wooded area.

The sinking sun painted the western sky aglow with pinks and oranges, tree branches creating black silhouettes reaching for the stars.

"Looks like something in an art museum." Was a tear welling in his eye? Karen's love of art had penetrated Jack's hard exterior, left him with a strange sensibility.

The night air was full of crispness, pine, and silence as they strolled toward the hotel and the promise of a night's rest before their final visit to Renate.

Chapter 29

The next morning, Jack and Sherk ate a substantial breakfast at the hotel, then drove to Renate's apartment. Mist dampened the air as Jack emerged from the car and breathed in the cool, green smell of leaves and moisture. He clutched the journal as if he didn't want to let it go. Well, he didn't.

"Guten Morgen," Renate greeted them as she answered their knock. "Kommt herein, kommt herein." She beamed, and led them to the sofa, offering the usual coffee and cake.

"Nein danke, wir haben gerade gefrühstückt," Sherk declined, explaining they just ate breakfast.

Renate's cheeks flushed pink, highlighting her azure eyes and rosy lips. She wore a dark green silky blouse over fitted white pants. She must've been a looker back in the war years.

She spoke with Sherk for a couple minutes as she eyed the journal on Jack's lap. Sherk turned to him. "Renate wonders if your dad wrote a lot of personal things, or mainly about the war. I told her it was about the Dachau liberation more than anything else."

Jack retrieved the photo from his pocket. "Should we show this to her?"

"Sure." Sherk took the snapshot and handed it to Renate while speaking to her.

She held it close to her face, tears welling in her eyes. "Ah, meine Güte." Renate touched her cheek with the photo. Then, without taking her eyes off the picture, she spoke in German, softly, transfixed.

Sherk leaned close to concentrate on Renate's words. When she'd finished, he turned to Jack.

"She remembers Bill taking this picture. It was at a picnic one afternoon by the river. She has happy memories of those times, but many townswomen were put on rubble duty for weeks after the war.

They had to help clean up streets and sidewalks by standing in lines and hauling away debris and wreckage from the bombings."

Sherk paused while Renate continued. He looked at Jack. "Since she and Ariana were needed at the hospital, they weren't recruited for the rubble brigade."

"Does she want to keep the photo?" Jack glimpsed at her.

"No, she has a copy of it, but hadn't seen it in years. Should I show her Ariana's part of the journal now? I'd guess she hasn't seen it, since she'd assume the whole thing was written in English by your dad."

Jack looked at Renate. She still studied the photo, running her spindly finger across the edge. He saw the wonder in her eyes. This was her family history too. "Yeah," Jack said. "But then try and convince her to let me keep it."

"Right." Sherk spoke to Renate, while Jack handed her the journal. She found Ariana's pages and began reading.

They sat in silence until she closed the notebook and looked up. "Es macht mich traurig." She pressed on speaking to Sherk.

Jack was getting cold feet. What if she refused to give up the journal? He could hardly tear the thing away from a tiny old lady.

Sherk turned to Jack. "She said she hadn't read Ariana's part before, and it makes her sad. She was aware of the relationship with your dad, since she and Ariana lived and worked together, and they'd always been close. Give me another minute while I see about you keeping the journal."

Moving closer, Sherk placed his hand on Renate's arm, speaking in quiet tones. Her brows furrowed, and her eyes darted between Jack and the journal still in her hands.

"Ah, ich weiss nicht—" she frowned as she went on, the journal clutched against her chest, her fingers white-knuckled.

Jack was like a deflated balloon. He pictured himself returning home with a stack of photocopies in a manila folder. Not good enough. He deserved the very pages his father had held in his hands. He deserved the original.

Renate's phone rang on the end table beside her chair. She looked annoyed, as she checked the caller ID. "Ah." Speaking to Sherk, she picked up the phone, smiled, and talked.

"It's Ariana's daughter from Stuttgart," Sherk whispered.

Renate's voice elevated to a near shrill; she seemed agitated.

After hanging up, she talked to Sherk. Jack thought he understood "Monika" mentioned in the conversation. A frown replaced her earlier smile. Jack figured she was upset, but he was no expert on women of any age.

"Looks like we'll have company," Sherk said. "Ariana's daughter Monika is in town on business, and got out early from her meeting. She decided to pop in for a visit with her mother and Renate, who had to make up a reason why we're here. Monika doesn't know about your dad or the journal. So, for the record, we're relatives of old friends of Renate's husband, whose name was Ewald Hahn."

"Right, I'm sure I'll keep that straight." Jack cleared his throat. "So, what about the journal?"

Sherk grimaced. "She's balking at giving it up. She promised Ariana it would go to the daughter, but she gave way a little. She can understand why you'd want it."

At that moment, she thrust the journal towards Jack. She turned, speaking to Sherk. He nodded. "Now she wants you to take it." He lowered his voice. "She didn't want the daughter to find out about it, and if you're holding it, she won't be rude and question a stranger about what's in his hands."

Jack shrugged. "Okay by me."

"Monika will be here in a few minutes, and then we'll visit Ariana. We'll bid auf wiedersehn then."

"Does Renate realize we're heading back to Munich today?"

"Yes, and she wants to keep in touch, so I'll give her my contact info."

Grateful that Renate had given him the insight on his father, Jack would miss her charm and goodness. She reminded him of his little Irish grandmother who had died when he was a boy. The same gentle ways, same cheerful face, same coffee, similar cake, in that his grandma never made apple strudel.

Several minutes later, a knock followed with a chirpy "Hallo" prompted Renate to rise and walk to the door. ""Komm herein, mein Lieblig."

Jack and Sherk both stood. An attractive dark-haired woman hugged Renate and glided into the living room. She chatted away with her and glanced at the men.

So, this was Monika. Jack's first reaction was perhaps he'd like to stick around longer than planned. He took in her ivory satiny blouse and black tailored pants, the same slim body of Renate's. She looked to be in her fifties, a little younger than Jack, but the right age if he were looking. And damn, why shouldn't he look?

Renate nervously guided Monika into the room, introducing her to Sherk and then Jack. Monika shook their hands, and said to Jack, "It's so good to meet you. Renate's told me about you."

"Same here." He grinned. "It's nice someone else speaks English."

"I'll bet it is. I learned it in school, and I use it on my job."

Her brown sleek hair, gently threaded with gray, curtained her face; sapphire eyes gazed at Jack. She resembled Ariana except for her darker hair and something else Jack couldn't pinpoint.

Renate directed them to sit down, arms waving about like a maestro conducting his orchestra. "Wer will Kaffee?" she sang, her cheeks flushed. Were her hands shaking?

Everyone declined her offer, either in German or English.

Jack wasn't sure how long they'd sit conversing with Monika, but hell, she was easy on his eyes. No hurry as far as he was concerned. He noticed a ring on each hand, both with serious rocks that sparkled as she moved her hands on her thighs. He willed himself to use his brain. After all, she lived overseas, and with his luck, married. Nevertheless, he found her intriguing, but off-limits.

Figuring it wouldn't hurt to be social, he said, "You mentioned you speak English in your job. What do you do?"

"I've worked for Mercedes for years," she said, with barely a German accent. "You may know Mercedes is headquartered in Stuttgart, and I teach English to German executives, as well as German to Americans and other expats who locate here for a while."

Jack nodded. "Interesting job. Have you been to the States?"

"A few times." Her dark blue eyes held his gaze as if they saw right through him. "My father had cousins in Texas, and we visited them a couple times."

His interest piqued. "Where in Texas? I lived near Houston for a few years."

"Really? We were in Dallas. I also was in New York City for a business trip a while ago." She brushed her hair behind her ears, raised her eyebrows in question. "According to Renate, you and Sherk are old friends of Ewald's family?"

Jack had to remember the story. "Yeah, kind of shirttail relations of friends."

She frowned. "Shirttail what?"

He gave a slight chuckle. "Oh, that means not real close relatives like parents and siblings, more like eighth cousins seven times removed, or something similar." Jack expected his joke to prompt a laugh. Instead, Monika only looked confused.

After an awkward moment, she grinned. "Okay, I guess I still haven't learned all the expressions of your language."

"No worries." Jack tried to look away but, damn, she was attractive. Her face had a subtle melancholy beauty, like her mother's. He wished he could take her out for lunch, but figured that wouldn't work. He'd have to drag Sherk along.

Just then, Sherk, who'd been engaged in conversation with Renate, turned to them. "Renate wants to see Ariana now, Jack. We can leave for the hotel after that."

Monika stood and started toward the door, talking to Renate.

Jack held the journal on his lap. "I guess I'll take this along?"

Sherk paused, lowered his voice. "Yeah, and then after Ariana's, we'll bid farewell and leave."

Sherk gave Jack a sideways glance. Had Renate confided something else to him? What more could there possibly be to learn? With Monica in earshot, Jack kept quiet. He could use a score card for who spoke what language. He took the journal and followed the rest out the door.

Renate still seemed flustered as she led the way to Ariana's unit, chatting with Monika.

"I hope Mutti's having a good day," Monika said, glancing backward at Jack. She adjusted the strap on her brown and black patterned bag. No doubt a designer purse. Jack wondered if her life was as manicured as her pale pink fingernails.

CHAPTER 30

When they reached Ariana's apartment, Renate knocked softly on the door. A woman's voice called, "Komm herein."

Monika opened the door, and they all traipsed into the room behind her. A familiar rosewater fragrance floated from the room. Jack recognized the same nurse's aide from several days ago, who bent close to Ariana, spoke to her in a child-like tone, and left the room. Renate bustled about, directing people where to sit.

Ariana sat perched on her bed, like a sparrow. Shiny silver hair framed her face. Jack thought of his father's 'peaches and cream' comment in his journal. Wrinkles etched on her complexion failed to hide clear, smooth skin. Her doe-like eyes darted back and forth between Monika and Renate. Once again, she reminded Jack of an aging Ingrid Bergman.

Jack sat in a chair by the bed, placing the journal close to his side. He sat silently while the whole room chattered away, catching a word now and then he understood, like 'Schröder, München, Haus'.

Monika sat by her mother, stroking her hands and speaking softly. Ariana seemed to recognize her daughter, smiling and nodding. Renate joined in the conversation in the same nervous-pitched voice.

Jack wondered what had happened to Renate's calm, cheerful disposition, but since Monika understood English, he hesitated mentioning it Sherk.

Monika spoke to Renate, her words rising in question.

"Ach—" Renate went on chattering to Monika, who shrugged and looked at Jack. "I asked her why she seems nervous, but she insists everything's fine." She must've read Jack's mind. They were already soul mates.

Renate turned to Sherk and spoke to him, clearing her throat now and then.

Sherk stood. "Jack, she wants me to step outside with her for a few minutes. She has questions about her husband's Hahn relatives and wants to get our contact information before we leave."

After Renate and Sherk left the room, Monika said, "I'm sure it's confusing having people talking away in German non-stop." She raised her eyebrows. "I wonder why Renate seems so high-strung today."

Jack shrugged, and switched the journal by his other side, hoping Monika wouldn't notice.

She sidled toward Jack's chair, still holding her mother's hand. "It's been so hard to see her mind fade away," she whispered, as though out of respect for her mother's long-lost sensibilities. "She seems a little worse every time I see her."

"I'm sorry," Jack said. "I had an uncle in Ireland who had Alzheimer's, and it was tough to see." He was amazed at how easily he could speak to Monika, like he'd known her for years.

"Yes, I figured you were Irish from your name. Have you been to Ireland?" She brushed imaginary lint from her pants.

Jack inwardly cringed, his thoughts flashing to twelve years ago. "Yeah." He lowered his eyes.

Monika's smile faded. "I'm sorry, I didn't mean to pry."

"That's okay. You didn't pry, it was a bad time in my life, a long story." He wouldn't have minded telling her the story of Karen and Elizabeth, but now wasn't the time. Having drinks in a quiet bar would be more suitable.

Monika nodded. "Yes, we all have stories, don't we?" She turned to her mother, who began humming a tune vaguely familiar to Jack. "Ah, Mutti—" Monika continued speaking in German.

Something clicked in Jack's brain. The humming melody sounded like a song Ariana mentioned in the journal. Might be his imagination, but damn, he couldn't hint at anything. The journal was a secret. He clenched it tightly, in an automatic reflex.

"She used to sing that song a lot," Monika glanced back at Jack. "She memorized all the words; it was popular during the war. She told me Bing Crosby sang it."

Something tugged in Jack's gut. "Yeah, it sounds a little familiar."

Monika kept on talking about her mother and Renate's closeness through the years, and her own life in Stuttgart, but she avoided personal subjects. No mention of a husband or kids, so—

"When do you go back to Chicago?" She shifted position on the bed.

Jack tried to read her body language, but no luck. Terrific. One more language he didn't understand. "We leave in a few days, on Tuesday morning," he replied.

Was Monika making polite conversation, or does she actually care?

"Oh, so soon?" She pouted, either mocking him or clearly disappointed. Jack chose the latter.

Before he could answer, the door opened and Renate and Sherk walked in, the usual German tongue filling the air. They both seemed anxious and ready to leave. Sherk brushed his hair from his forehead.

"We'll be on our way now, Jack. Renate's ready to go and give Monika some time alone with her mother."

"Well, I guess, but—" Jack wondered why the hurry. He had been on the verge of inviting Monika for drinks later, assuming he'd get up the nerve.

Renate spoke to Ariana and gave her a quick hug.

Monika stood and straightened the collar of her silky blouse. "It was so nice meeting you two." She shook Sherk's hand, then Jack's. He noted the warmth in her expression.

"Same here," Jack said. Did she let her hand linger in his, or did he imagine it? "Maybe we'll meet again sometime."

"I'd like that very much." She let go of his hand, but, for a split second, not his eyes.

Sherk tried to drag him from the room, voicing their goodbyes. Jack glimpsed at Ariana, who looked at him, and hummed louder, with occasional words blended in. He followed Sherk's lead and bent down close to her, whispering goodbye.

Ariana grasped Jack's hand and stared at his face. "Die—die Drossel." She moaned. "Die—die—" Her moaning persisted, mouth turned downward, eyes moistened.

Monika frowned. "Mutti, was meinst du—"

Sherk whispered to Jack that she asked Ariana what she meant by moaning about a bluebird.

Renate piped in and spoke to Monika. Again, Sherk told Jack that she claimed the groaning didn't mean anything, and Ariana had said 'bluebird' before.

Renate tried to hustle the men towards the door, but Ariana's grasp on Jack's hand tightened. Monika gently pried it away.

She shrugged. "I wonder why she's whining about a bluebird all of a sudden, except it was always her favorite."

Jack's brain clicked. Bluebird. Once again, he apparently triggered the memory.

Sherk said to Monika, "That's the reason she mentioned it, then. Her favorite bird. Come on, Jack." He turned. "Monika—" he spoke to her in German, and followed Renate out the door, Jack trailing behind, journal in hand. He turned toward Monika, reluctant, grappling for an excuse to stay one more minute, one more second. Probably making an ass of himself. The door swung closed behind him.

They reached Renate's apartment, but only stayed a few minutes. She and Sherk spoke. She looked at the notebook in Jack's hand.

"She wants you to keep it, Jack." Sherk said. "She doesn't plan to tell Monika about the affair with John. She insists it wouldn't benefit her, and her promise to Ariana is a moot point, due to her mental state. I agree, not that my humble opinion matters."

Jack sighed in relief. "Okay, great. Copies wouldn't be the same as the real thing anyway."

He took Renate's hand and held it. "Thank you so much for everything." Jack turned to Sherk. "She won't understand me, so will you tell her how grateful I am that she told us her story and how it will help my brother and me understand our father." He was turning into a nice guy.

"She knows, Jack." He nodded to Renate. "Look at her."

Jack turned to Renate, who beamed at him. "Leb wohl, bis wir uns wiedersehen."

He returned her smile. "Auf Wiedersehen." He leaned down and gave her a quick hug.

"Congratulations, my friend." Sherk placed his hand on Jack's shoulder. "You've mastered the universal language of gratitude and farewell."

She opened the door, and Jack sensed her watching as they walked down the corridor. His time with Renate was over.

Now all he had to do is figure out a way to see Monika again.

CHAPTER 31

"Seems this is my lucky day," Jack said as he and Sherk drove to the hotel. "I get to keep the journal and I meet an interesting woman."

Sherk didn't answer, his eyes glued to the road.

"Everything okay?" Jack wondered if Sherk had bad news from Erica. Maybe she'd texted him earlier.

"Yeah, why?"

"You and Renate were acting like nervous cats. What gives?"

"Nothing." Sherk looked straight ahead, jaw twitching.

Jack didn't buy the comment, but he'd let it go. They drove in silence for several minutes. "Anyway, I enjoyed meeting Monika. Nice woman, and good looking too."

"Yes, she's very pleasant, but—" Sherk slowed down to turn into the parking lot of the Leonardo Hotel.

"But what?"

"Nothing." Sherk parked the car and glanced out the window.

"You're like a broken record. What's on your mind?" Jack opened the door and stepped out.

"We'll talk in the room," Sherk said as they walked through circular front doors. "Then we'll pack and take off."

"Already?" He wanted to see Monika again. A quick drink before she left for Stuttgart?

"We need to get back to Munich." They reached Sherk's room. "Come on in."

Jack sank down on the armchair by the TV. "I may be crazy, but I thought about talking to Monika again—"

Sherk sat on the bed. "Well, I'll tell you, we need to—" He drew in a deep breath.

Jack's eye twitched. "Yeah, right. But the first time in years I meet someone I want to see again, probably younger, but not by much, I can't see—"

"Well, she lives across the ocean from you, Jack." Sherk's mouth quivered at the sides.

"I'm aware of that." Jack said, irritated. "What's the big deal? Is she married? I never did find out."

"It just isn't a good idea. Ah, well, we must—" Frown lines appeared between his brows.

"Gotta tell ya, man, I'm losing what little patience I have. Why not tell me, 'Gee, you finally meet a woman you like. Go ahead and see her again.'" Jack stood and walked to the window.

Sherk sighed. "Because it's not a good idea—" He scratched his chin.

"You said that already. I got it the first time." Jack's blood pressure rose along with his voice. "Come on, spit it out. What's your problem?" He started pacing.

"Okay, you can't date Monika, Jack."

"Why the hell not?" He almost shouted.

"Because—because—" He clenched his jaw.

"Come on, out with it, man. Because why?"

Sherk moved close to Jack and locked eyes with him.

"Because she's your sister."

CHAPTER 32

Jack stared back at Sherk. His fists clenched. "Huh?" He couldn't register the words. Stunned, he squinted, shaking his head.

"Actually, she's your half-sister, and I'll tell you the story after you—"

"You're fulla' shit, man. That woman is younger than me, how did Pa—he left a year after the war, then Tommy—he never went back to Germany—" Jack's blood drained from his face.

Sherk sighed. "Sit down, Jack, and take some deep breaths." He reached for a mini whisky bottle on the cabinet. "Here, have a shot or two. Or a beer."

Jack walked to the window and back. "Still it makes no sense, Monika is—" He swiped strands of hair off his temple.

"Actually, she's a few months older than Tommy. She just looks younger, her skin—"

"Jesus, Mary, and Joseph. I'll take that shot now." Jack took the glass, gulped one drink, then poured another. He sat in the chair and wiped his forehead, crossing and uncrossing his legs. "Okay, tell me the story, which I take it Renate told you when she took you out of Ariana's room for your private talk."

Sherk nodded. "Yes, a real surprise. I thought Monika was younger too. Obviously has her mother's genes, which many Germans are notable for—"

"Okay, Führer, don't tell me about your frickin' superior race right now." Jack tried to pull the words back. Too late. Weighed down by shock, disappointment, and now shame, his head dropped.

"I'm sorry," he mumbled.

Sherk said nothing, but helped himself to a beer, sat on the bed, and cleared his throat. "All right, here's the story. I need to keep everything straight, so bear with me."

Jack's pulse quickened as he downed his second shot.

"When Ariana and your dad were involved, she told Renate almost everything." Sherk popped the cap off the beer and drank. "When your father left for home, it was around mid-June of 1946, almost two weeks after his last journal entry. A week or so later, she wrote in the last pages and hid the journal away. Then in July, she suspected she was pregnant, and a week or two later was sure." Sherk adjusted his glasses. "She figured it happened in May. By that time, of course, your dad had left, so she talked to Renate. Of course, Ariana was upset, couldn't decide what to do. Meanwhile this Walter Gunther, her friend from childhood, had always fancied her and still lived in their neighborhood."

Jack stared straight ahead.

Sherk placed his hand on Jack's shoulder. "Jack, you following me?"

Jack nodded.

Sherk persisted. "But she didn't have romantic sentiment for this guy, especially after meeting your father. Anyway, he'd been hanging around after John left for the States, and one day she blurted out to Walter that she was in a mess and ended up telling him about the pregnancy. Right away he offered to marry her. Long story short, he accepted the fact she wasn't in love with him, but he was happy to be her husband and raise her little girl as his own. They kept it a secret, even from their parents. Only Renate knew the truth."

Jack frowned. "Didn't anyone suspect, since she and Walter hadn't been dating until they suddenly got married?"

"Renate said her mother and other people just figured they conceived the baby before the wedding. Back then, ordinary couples didn't have big church weddings with brides in white gowns. They were married in an office somewhere with only the family around. Remember, the whole country was still recovering from the war, and people were walking around shell shocked. Things weren't back to normal by a long shot."

"I'll be damned." Jack shook his head. "You sure Monika doesn't have a clue?"

Sherk took a drink of beer. "Renate swears she doesn't. She always thought of Walter Gunther as her father. Ariana was going to tell her someday, but the right time never came. Then after Walter died, she got busy with other things, and later started slipping into dementia."

A thought occurred to Jack. His father, who had seen more and loved more than Jack could have ever suspected, had also lost more: a daughter he never knew he had.

"And Ariana never told Pa." He spoke his words to the puckered carpet.

"No." Sherk replied. "She wanted to, but decided it would hurt him and your mother, and what could he do about it? She didn't want to ruin John's family, your family."

"What about the letter we found in the box? Did she figure she was pregnant when she wrote it?" Jack was still trying to let this bombshell sink in.

"Renate wasn't sure. She thought Ariana told her in July sometime, and the letter was written July 14, so it's possible. But she didn't hint at it unless that's what she meant when she said she was damaged. But I'm positive she meant the assault, not being pregnant. I don't know, Jack. No one ever will."

Jack thought for a minute. "It shouldn't be a huge surprise, it happens a lot in wartime, but when it's you, a different story." He'd tell Tommy for sure. He had a right, but should they tell their other siblings they have a half-sister in Germany?

"That's true," Sherk agreed. "Countless children were left behind in wartime throughout history."

"Yeah. And I was ready to take Monika out for a drink. I was sure she was younger." Then it dawned on him. It had been something about the shape of Monika's nose, the curve of her jaw, that struck him as familiar. "Oddly enough, or not, her profile kind of resembles Jenny's."

Sherk shrugged. "Could be. I've only met your sister a couple times, but perhaps so. He paused. "We should pack and hit the road."

Jack stood. "In a way, I'd like to see Monika for a goodbye again. Or do I? Hell, I dunno what to make of all this."

"You sure about that?" Sherk frowned. "Remember, she doesn't know. She might assume you're seeing her again for different reasons."

Jack's shoulders dropped. Sherk was right. Seeing Monika would be selfish.

Sherk apparently accepted Jack's resignation. He opened the door. "I'll see you in a few minutes after we're packed."

Jack headed for his room. Still hard to comprehend the attractive woman he'd met earlier was his half-sister. One thing for sure, his mother must never discover the truth. It would send her to an early grave. No easy answer. What is the boundary between a person's right to the truth and the right to keep painful secrets? Damned if he could tell.

CHAPTER 33
Chicago – late June 2012

A week later, Jack sat in his living room waiting for Tommy to show up. Boone, his aging yellow dog of mixed heritage, lay at his feet snoring gently. Jack and Sherk had arrived in Chicago after the long flight, during which they sat mostly in silence, a comfortable silence achieved only by friends who had transcended awkwardness. The Germany trip had certainly broadened and transformed Jack's perspective of the world and human nature.

Although the trip was an eye-opener, and successful because it had solved the mystery of Ariana's letter, Jack was glad to return to his comfortable duplex in Bridgeport, a once-working-class Irish community on Chicago's south side.

The Uber ride from the airport had been a real culture shock. As they sped along the freeway, all he saw were Home Depot and Best Buy mega stores. Twenty minutes later, the old Sears Tower, now the Willis, loomed high, piercing the skyline, and as they approached Bridgeport, the modern glass and chrome architecture of the Illinois Institute of Technology gleamed in pale orange sunlight.

Yes, he would miss the ancient churches and fortresses of Munich, not to mention the hospitality of Sherk's relatives. He'd wanted to buy them a gift of appreciation, but Sherk dismissed the idea. *Just treat them to dinner sometime, Jack. They don't need a thing.*

The last day they had planned to visit the Dachau museum and camp, but as they approached the area, Jack had said, "Sorry, pal, gonna have to bail. Just can't hack the idea of walking through the place. I'll tell Ma some general things about it. God knows, I learned plenty from the journal."

•　　　•　　　•　　　•　　　•

Leaning back on his well-worn leather recliner, he thought of the knowledge Sherk had bestowed upon him. Yes, he would miss the old cathedrals and palaces of Munich.

Sherk had spoken about the collective guilt and denial of many German people that exists even to this day. He had absorbed many comments through past years from his relatives and friends, and said how complicated it all was and still remains. "It's always a sore spot with me," Sherk had told him, "when people allege the Germans had to know the truth about the Jews and camps, and how could the country allow such horror to come about?"

Jack had responded, "Yeah, what could ordinary people do if they saw the violence? Call the cops, who were the Gestapo? Then they themselves would've ended up like Ariana's dad, thrown in Dachau or worse."

Sherk had explained that people who opposed the Reich chose to be killed or imprisoned, and the world didn't learn who they were. People like Ariana's father. But most folks back then didn't go out and protest in the streets when their Jewish neighbors were beaten or carted away. They chose to live. Live for themselves and their families.

Jack recalled Sherk's words. "I've wondered myself if I'd risk my life, knowing my death wasn't going to save anyone else's life. Did Emil Schröder's death help anything? It didn't save the life of any Jew, gypsy, gay person. Perhaps he thought he had to sacrifice his life for his principles. I don't have the answer. Did that make him a hero or a fool?"

"Damn good question," Jack had said. "But I don't have the negative view I once had of the Germans. The criminals were individuals. Not a whole country."

•   •   •   •   •

Deep in thought, Jack sprang to life when Boone's thunderous bark broke the silence. Tommy had rung the doorbell, right on time as usual. Although the dog was nearly thirteen years old, he guarded the house like an armed sentry.

"Come on in." Jack shook his brother's hand and gave his back a light slap. This was the typical extent of the Bailey show of affection, but now, Jack hesitated and gave his brother an actual hug.

Obviously surprised, Tommy backed away. "Welcome back." He came in and headed for the sofa. Slightly shorter than Jack, he was heavier around the middle. His black hair, liberally salted with gray, was shaved close to his head. People spotted the family resemblance between the two, since they both looked rugged and world-weary at times.

"Is Ma back from Saint Paul yet?" Jack led Tommy into the living room.

"No, next week. Tuesday, so you have a little time before the inquisition," Tommy joked.

"How 'bout a Guinness?" Jack made his way to the kitchen, glancing back at his brother.

"Sure," Tommy answered as he rubbed Boone's back and settled on the couch. "Been chomping at the bit to discover everything and read the journal. I get the drift there's something you haven't mentioned."

"You'll see. Patience, my man." Jack returned with the dark beer and set the bottles on the pine coffee table on coasters he'd swiped from the Hofbräuhaus. He sat beside Tommy, journal in hand. "Well, where do you want to start?"

Tommy nodded at the journal. "I'll start with that, since you've kept me posted about Renate and her story." Jack handed him the notebook. Tommy stared at its worn brown cover, turning it front to back. He opened the beginning pages. "Yeah, that's Pa's handwriting." He took his eyes from the page and gazed straight ahead. "I can't wrap my head around this. Like his ghost has come back."

"You're tellin' me." Jack reached for the worn black-and-white photo on the end table. "By the way, here's the picture I told you about."

Tommy held it close and squinted at the image of a young soldier, his arm around a lovely girl. "So that's Ariana. Gotta admit, she was a good lookin' broad. I can see why the old man wanted to—never mind. Better hide this where Ma will never see it." He handed the snapshot back to Jack.

"Yeah, it'll be hidden away with the journal." Jack stood. "I'll take Boone out for a short walk. Let you read in peace. See ya in a while." He looped the dog's leash around his neck, took one last glance at his brother who had already become lost in their father's words. Jack let the door click to a close behind him.

•　　　•　　　•　　　•　　　•

Within half an hour, chilled from the wonderfully familiar Chicago wind, Jack and Boone returned from their walk. Tommy still sat with the journal in his hands. "God, that's some story. I had no idea the old man lived through all that. The Dachau camp was unreal. To see it first-hand like that. No wonder he drank like an effen' fish." Tommy's eyes drifted somewhere far way. "How would you ever erase that stuff from your mind? Even as cops, we never saw anything close to that. Hell, no wonder you didn't visit the camp. Got more than enough reading this."

"Beats me. I'll tell ya, man, I learned more the last three weeks than the last ten years."

Jack unleashed Boone, gave him a milk bone treat, and brought two more beers to the table, ignoring the empty bottles. Plenty of German coasters on hand.

Tommy handed Jack the journal. "Can you remember much about Ariana's writing in the back? You said Sherk could translate for me some time, but wonder if you could recall any of it."

Jack thumbed through the pages. "You can see Pa's name off and on, and here's Bing Crosby's name when she's talking about songs they liked. Pa sang to her sometimes."

"You're shittin' me," Tommy exclaimed. "He sang to her? Jesus, all I remember is him on a bender, stumbling around belting out "Oh Danny Boy, the pipes, the pipes are calling. Then he'd forget the words and get pissed about it."

Jack scoffed. "Yeah, then he'd start wailing, 'I'll take you home again Maureen, across the ocean wild and leave ya there.' He'd roar like hell, and Ma would pretend to get mad, and he'd get more off-key."

"Those were the days." Tommy gazed at the last page. "What does the signature part read?"

"Guess what. They're lyrics from "April Showers". She writes she'll always—wait, let me see. I can translate this, because I remember the words. Here goes:

So keep on looking for a bluebird
And list'ning for his song
Whenever April showers come along

John, my darling, may we always see a bluebird.

My love, always and forever,

Your Sweetheart"

"Holy crap," said Tommy. "That was written for John Bailey? Our old man?"

"I told ya. We're in the twilight zone." Jack looked at his brother shaking his head in disbelief. This was as good a time as any. "I still haven't revealed the real deal. Are you ready?"

"What else could there be? On second thought, did Pa leave any, ah, souvenirs behind?"

"Well—"

"Come on, Jack, out with it."

Jack closed the journal. Should he spit it out or do a prologue? "You remember when I gave you updates on Renate's diary, and that Ariana had a husband and daughter?"

Tommy nodded slowly, grimaced. "How old is her daughter?"

"I met her the last day in Weimar, her name is Monika, and I thought she was younger than me."

"But," Tommy said, his impatience growing.

"You guessed it. She's actually a few months older than you." Jack raised his brows.

Tommy inhaled. "Christ. She's John's kid. Our half-sister." It wasn't a question.

"Yup. Hard to pull the wool over your eyes," Jack said. "You don't seem as shocked as I was."

"Well, it was war. Not unusual. Anyway, did you get a picture of her? Monika?" The diatribe of questions poured from him. "What does she look like? Does she know Pa was her father?"

"Whoa, you'll find out everything, but no picture, and she reminded me of Jenny after I found out. She's totally unaware of the affair, so she's in the dark about, well, about everything."

Jack explained the timeline to Tommy, how Walter Gunther wanted to marry Ariana, raise the baby as his own, how they never had more children. How Renate had always wondered about that, but Ariana had told her Monika's delivery was difficult, and she didn't want to go through childbirth again.

Tommy rubbed his forehead. "Okay. We need to decide whether to tell the others. Not Ma, of course. I'm still not sure she never saw the letter. But she'd keel over if she got wind of Monika. Pa with another daughter. Holy shit."

"Yeah, I'll keep the journal under lock and key. I can't decide about telling the kids either. Sherk and I talked about it a little. I'd wanna be told. Andy and Jenny would be okay with it. Mike hasn't been around for years, and that's not something you text about."

"We'll contemplate it. No need to make a quick decision," Tommy said.

"Right. I'll see if Sherk can meet us next week. We can run things by him, and I want him to tell you more about the trip."

Tommy raised his eyebrows. "You taking life advice from Sherk now?'

"Sherk's…" Jack paused. There was no way to explain the bond he and Sherk had formed on their trip. "He's a wise man, good common sense, plus he'd be more unbiased than we are. I'd like to know his thoughts."

"Okay, it's getting late." Tommy stood and stretched. "Time flies when you find out you have more relatives than you thought."

Night had closed in and darkness wrapped itself around the city as Tommy left for his house.

Jack watched his brother drive away. Would Tommy be more sympathetic and forgiving after discovering what their father had gone through? He hadn't addressed the topic, but Bailey men weren't renowned for their emotional disclosure.

Perhaps both he and Tommy could now see John Bailey as a young soldier who saw the worst of humanity, a scarred liberator, unable to exorcize his own demons until death.

CHAPTER 34

Several days later, Jack walked through the door of Shinnick's Pub, eager to meet Tommy and Sherk for an early dinner and talk over the revelations from the Germany trip. As he'd hoped, it was too early for an evening crowd, relatively quiet. A few other customers mingled around the bar area.

"Hey, Bailey, long time no see," a man of sizeable proportions called out.

Jack headed toward the bar. "Charlie, good to see ya. Got a Guinness ready?" The place was an old-time watering hole, with dark wood, a traditional bar with brass and mirrors, shelves displaying bottles and glasses of all shapes and sizes.

Charlie, the amiable bartender, had poured drinks at Shinnick's for decades and prided himself in being pals with both Mayor Daleys, who grew up in Bridgeport and were no strangers to the pub.

"Comin' right up." Yellow bar lights reflected off Charlie's glistening head as he filled a mug, foaming brew spilling down the sides.

"The mayor been in lately?" Jack never tiring of reminding Charlie of the good ol' days when Chicago's upstanding public servants held sway.

"Nah, haven't seen hide nor hair of him since he got too uppity for us and moved north, left his old stomping grounds in the lurch."

"Charlie, that was twenty years ago, not last week." Jack picked up his glass.

"Harrumph," Charlie scoffed and glanced toward the door. "Looks like ya got company."

Jack turned and saw Sherk and Tommy traipsing inside. "Well, look what the cat drug in," he said to Charlie.

"Hey," Charlie beamed. "I got two Baileys here. My lucky day. You guys up for a Guinness?"

"Sure thing, Charlie," Tommy said. "Burgers and fries too." The men made their way to a booth in the far corner.

"Ma should be home by now, Jack, so brace yourself."

"Yeah, with luck I'll get by with just an hour of interrogation." He admitted to himself that he'd miss the old girl if she weren't around.

Twenty minutes later, the glasses sat precariously close to empty. Jack turned toward the bar, intending to beckon Charlie. But no need; the cavalry was already on its way.

Charlie ambled toward their booth with plates of burgers, fries, and another round of beer.

Jack half-nodded. God, it was good to be home.

"Sorry we're all outta kale, Sherk," Charlie said, setting the plates down. "Just hafta eat unhealthy tonight." He walked away, guffawing at his own wit.

"Smells great. I was hungrier than I thought." Tommy took a bite of his juicy burger.

Sherk cut his in half. "You guys help yourselves to fries."

"Aw, live a little, man. They won't kill ya." The words trailed away as Jack immediately regretted his comment. Dumb thing to blab to a man whose wife had cancer.

"I'll live dangerously and eat a few." Sherk looked at Tommy. "Have you processed everything you learned from Jack and reading your dad's journal?"

Tommy finished chewing and set his burger down. "Yeah, I'm getting there. The main question for Jack and me is whether to tell the siblings about Monika. It's a tough decision."

Jack said, "I kinda want to tell them. If it were me, and I didn't know about a half-sister somewhere, I'd wanna find out. Not sure what I'd do with the info though. Look her up?" He shrugged.

Sherk rested his fork on the plate. "The question is are they better off with the truth or not? Did you read where they just launched a DNA ancestry service where you can look up your relatives from far and wide? More and more people will research their families, and Monika could very well do that sometime."

Jack frowned. "Renate must be aware of DNA, and how Monika could someday find out she had another father."

"I'm not sure," Tommy said. "This is a new concept, and if Renate keeps up with the news, she'd be worried. Anyway, it would be her decision to tell Monika, not ours."

Jack thought. "I suppose. But again, does she have the right to know about her real father?"

"We could debate this forever," Sherk said. "For now, you need to decide about your siblings. If you wait too long to tell them, they'll be upset and wonder why you didn't tell them as soon as you got back."

Jack and Tommy glanced at each other, nodding their agreement. Tommy wiped his mouth with his napkin. "We need to set a deadline. Either tell them in a week or two or forget it."

"Okay," Jack said. He glanced at a calendar on his phone. "Let's agree July fifteenth at the latest."

"Right," Tommy said. "Sherk, you're our witness. By the way, how did your relatives cope after the war? Jack's told me about your grandfather and his family. How nice they were to him."

Sherk pushed his plate aside. "They did okay, no worse than lots of folks. Like a lot of Germans, they don't talk about it. Opa won't reveal anything at all, but Oma will talk about waiting in lines for food, and drinking a kind of tea she didn't like. She still has the old red stool she'd bring to sit on in the queue. Actually, Renate spoke more about her life than anyone I've met from that generation."

Jack waved a fry at Tommy. "You'd be amazed. Germans back in the thirties were just like us. They went to school, played games, had friends, but I'm not sure about those fairy tales. Pretty dark."

Sherk chuckled. "Ah, the Struwwelpeter stories...*But Pauline said, oh what a pity, for when they burn it is so pretty.* It sums up people giving in to false promises."

"So, I guess most Germans were aware of what actually happened?" Tommy said. "But figured they couldn't do anything about it?"

Sherk nodded. "The age-old question. It depends who you talk to. Many people didn't consider Nazism as evil, after 1933 in particular. Their lives were better after the economic depression, far worse than it was here in America. Their economy improved, largely due to rearmament and construction, people could work again, have better housing, even go on vacation, and could see doctors. Plus, the biggie of having their national pride restored after the humiliation of the Great War. People were ready for the rise of Germany. The New Order."

"Sounds like Ariana's family was happy then," Tommy said. "Other than their pa who knew and hated the truth about the Nazis."

"Yes," said Sherk. "People like him, the Social Democrats, were the ones who rebelled and were imprisoned or killed for it. Of course, they were anonymous, so no one found out about their sacrifice. Some boys in the Youth saw the experience as summer camping, parades, and the camaraderie of the Boy Scouts. The Nazis were experts at camouflaging their heinous beliefs behind carnivals, parades, rallies, things that everyone roots for, like our sports events."

Tommy drained his mug. "I don't get it. How? How could people not realize what was happening to the Jews and other so-called undesirables? They'd see them being carted off and put on trains."

"More propaganda." Sherk straightened his glasses. "There were newspaper reports that claimed Jewish men were taken into custody for their own protection, and were sent away for relocation."

Jack scoffed. "Who would buy that?"

"People who wanted to believe, or for whom it was convenient to believe," Sherk said. "Some insisted that Jews taken to the camps were traitors to Germany. The others were allowed to take their property or sell it at a fair price and leave the country. The Jews that were killed committed treason, in some Germans' minds." Sherk gave a slight cough. "I read where a good many citizen said the whole thing didn't happen. Even with photos of bodies, it wasn't proof. They claimed that Hitler had nothing to do with it. The violence was done by thugs, not him. One guy said that it was wrong, if it happened, but he wasn't convinced it happened."

"Yeah, totally amazed people can deny the Holocaust," said Tommy. "Takes all kinds."

"As for collective guilt," Sherk went on, "we should examine ourselves. Would you stand up and protest in those circumstances, risking your life, or would you choose to live? Your martyrdom wouldn't have helped the anti-Nazism, regardless."

Tommy shook his head. "People swear it couldn't happen again, and I tend to agree, but—"

Sherk said, "People are convinced the Nazi regime was an entire country gone mad, which makes it a little easier to agree it can't happen here. All we can do is hope, and do what we must."

"This has been very interesting," Tommy said. "Jack learned a lot from the trip, not only about our pa and Monika, but about ourselves too."

Sherk stood. "How about another round?"

"You bet," Jack said, and watched Sherk head toward the bar.

"You've got a good friend there, Jack." Tommy glanced away.

"You have no idea." A flush rose on Jack's face. "Told ya, he's a wise man. We plan to get together for drinks now and then. Don't wanna lose touch with him. I just hope his wife gets well."

They sat in silence for several seconds. Jack shifted in his seat. "Are you ready to let Pa off the hook for what kind of father he was?"

Tommy shrugged. "I guess a little. I figure seeing the gore and the shock of the camp, plus his combat, and then meeting a girl to ease the pain, then leaving her. I dunno. Was it the real thing with her, or was it because of the war?"

"Guess we'll never know. I never thought he and Ma had a marriage made in heaven."

"Right now, I do have a sense of relief or something. Knowing the old man suffered through that hell. I mean, not that I'm glad he experienced it," Tommy clarified. "But there was a reason for him becoming..." Jack waited as Tommy struggled for words. "The real shame is he never got help. He always refused to go to AA when Uncle Hank brought it up. He could've used a shrink too. But back then, veterans were heroes in the minds of America. They were tough. Didn't need help. The greatest generation, and all that."

"It's high time to give the past a rest, Tommy. And I reckon we've both put Pa to rest too.

We'll leave it to Renate to tell Monika or not. But Jenny and Andy and Mike have a right."

Sherk arrived with their drinks on a tray, and sat. "Charlie put me to work. The place is filling up."

"We'll have to do this again, Sherk," Tommy said. "This could be the beginning of a beautiful friendship."

Jack raised his glass.

"Here's lookin' at you, kid."

CHAPTER 35

The next morning Jack awoke to his phone buzzing on the nightstand. He glanced at the caller ID, groaned, and punched the speaker button. "Yeah, Ma. Do ya have an idea what time it is?" His digital clock glowered red in the dark.

"Don't get smart with me, Jacky. You know I just got back from Saint Paul yesterday. I was exhausted, but didn't sleep a wink last night, so I—"

"Okay. Okay What's on your mind?" As if he didn't know.

"Guess I can't expect you to casually mention, 'how was your trip?' Or 'how is Aunt Betty?' You haven't seen her in a coon's age."

Jack wanted to bury his head in the pillow. "Sorry, Ma. How's Aunt Betty?"

"Oh, don't ask. She's got a bad hip that really needs—never mind. I know you're bored." She paused to take a breath. "So why am I calling? When can you come over? I can't wait for you to tell me all about Germany. Did you visit Dachau? How was Sherk's house? Oh, did you—"

"Hold on, Ma. I can't talk now. I'll be over this afternoon. How 'bout around five?"

"How 'bout this morning? You can stay for lunch." Jack visualized her smoothing her bottle-fed henna hair.

"Yeah, okay. See ya at eleven. Bye, Ma." He clicked off before she could respond. Oh well, she was used to his impertinence. Wouldn't take it personally.

•　　•　　•　　•　　•

Jack parked his used black Beemer in front of his mother's house in an older neighborhood near Pershing Road, the southern boundary of

Bridgeport. The day was typical for late June, the sun bathing a blue sky and cool breezes floating through maple and oak trees lining streets and sidewalks.

Jack grew up in the three-level house, once dark green. Updated through the years, it now featured pale gray siding with light trim, a newly-painted white picket fence surrounding the small front yard. It struck him how much the place had transformed over time, similar in nature to his memories of his father evolving into something fresh and brighter.

Reaching the shiny black front door, Jack knocked twice and let himself in with the key he kept in his possession. "Home, Ma," he called out as a whiff of roasted chicken drifted from the kitchen.

"There you are, Jacky," Maureen Bailey warbled, as she bustled to the door to give Jack a hug. As though in a dream, he was transported back to Germany. What was it? Jack struggled to make the connection. Then it struck him. His mother sounded like Renate, the same welcoming sing-song voice.

Jack stepped back as his mother released him from the embrace. He looked at her with a new appreciation, something he couldn't explain. A woman of medium height and generous proportions, Maureen took pride in assuring her unnatural red curls were just so, and her clothes bright and colorful. No drab black or beige for her.

Taking in her emerald green top with sparkles round the collar, Jack said, "Just as beautiful as Ms. O'Hara."

Maureen harrumphed. "Well, I must declare, I try." Her lifelong comparison to the famed actress was a family joke. She enjoyed bragging they were born the same year.

Jack followed his mother into the kitchen, where the table was set for two. "We'll sit in here since there's only you and me. Tommy couldn't get away from work, or so he said."

Jack glanced at the bowls of steaming mashed potatoes, gravy, green beans with sesame seeds, soda bread. "Jeez, Ma, ya didn't have to make enough for an army. It's just lunch. What's wrong with a sandwich?"

She waved a dismissive hand at him and hustled about the stove and counter, then took a roasting pan of golden chicken from the oven. "Well, I always like lots of leftovers, and I'll send some home with you."

"I'll get the wine." Jack retrieved a bottle of chardonnay from the fridge, along with two glasses. He watched Maureen fussing over savory-looking chicken as he poured the wine. For no apparent reason, thoughts of Erica's battle with cancer and of Ariana's dementia entered his mind. Today, he decided, he would sit back, enjoy the meal, and count himself lucky his mother was still cooking at her age.

•   •   •   •   •

Thirty minutes later they sat in the living room finishing cherry pie, vanilla ice cream, and coffee. Maureen dabbed at her mouth with a napkin. "Well, that's all about my trip and Aunt Betty. Now what I've been waiting for. Tell me everything about Germany."

Figuring that wasn't going to happen, Jack said. "Okay, but I can't sit here all day, Ma. Got things to do."

She raised her eyebrows. "Like what?"

"Nothing." He paused. "Sherk's folks' house is right in Munich. Very handy to everything." Jack continued, but the description of his sightseeing and his visit to Sherk's grandparents in Regensburg struck him as superficial, a travel brochure without a mention of the destination's true purpose and ultimate revelation.

"Did you visit Dachau?" Maureen sipped her coffee.

"Yeah, but it's changed since Pa was there. Built up. A lot of it's a museum now, but some buildings are still standing."

She cringed when Jack mentioned the gas chambers and crematoriums. "Your father never would talk about it, but I know it stayed with him." Her gaze turned to the window. She was somewhere far away. "All his nightmares, you know."

Jack nodded. "Not to mention the booze and the belt on our backsides."

"Jacky." She looked at him with utter reproach. "You should realize the war caused all that. It wasn't his fault."

Jack dropped his head. "Yeah, okay." He had momentarily slipped into his former mindset of anger toward his pa. Now his mind had changed, but he'd always keep the journal with its details of the horrors of Dachau and Pa's affair with Ariana forever shielded from his mother.

Maureen stood and walked to an end table across the white and navy living room. It struck Jack like him, the room had changed. The shiny hard floors were a far cry from the avocado green shag carpet of Jack's boyhood.

"This is my favorite picture of your father and me." Maureen reached for a pewter-framed black-and-white photo of a young man in a long-sleeved shirt, his arm around a slim, attractive woman with shoulder-length curls. They stood in the front yard beside the same lilac bush that blooms today.

Jack drained his coffee and thought of another black and white snapshot of the same young man in his Army uniform, arm around another pretty girl.

"Yeah, I know, Ma. It was taken right after the war." The picture had been displayed on various tables in the house since Jack could remember.

"Is there anything else about Dachau to report or any other information?"

Jack avoided her gaze. Was she fishing? Did she suspect more?

"Nope, that's it." He stood and picked up his dessert place. "I'll see you soon. Gotta go."

He made his way toward the kitchen.

"Are you sure there wasn't anything else?" Maureen followed him, carrying her cup and plate.

"Yeah, Ma, I'm sure." He opened the dishwasher, loaded his plate, and placed the wine glass by the sink. Anything to avoid her eyes.

"You know, when he had his nightmares? He'd call out sometimes." She ran water in the sink. "Names."

Jack cleared his throat. "That right? Guess it's typical for soldiers after wartime."

"Names I never heard before. German words." Maureen rinsed the other plates and put them in the dishwasher. "I always meant to write down what they sounded like, but would forget in the morning."

"Oh. Well, just normal. He was around German words all the time, after the war especially." Jack wiped his brow, shuffled his feet. "Thanks for the lunch and — "

"He picked up some German when he was in Munich." She wiped her hands. "Ah yes. I remember my friends' husbands and sweethearts coming back the summer it all ended. The summer of forty-five. I didn't understand why your father — " her voice trailed off.

"I'm sure the waiting was hard, but at least you were convinced he was safe, right?"

"Oh yes, and he wrote letters home too. I wonder what ever happened to them." She turned, looked at Jack. "They must've gotten lost in the shuffle years ago. So much stuff in this house, with all you kids." She stopped. "Oh, not that I'm complaining. Not about you kids." She tittered.

Jack nodded. "Yeah, right." Not sure, but water under the bridge. He headed out of the kitchen. "See you soon, Ma. You haven't lost your touch at the cookstove."

"And another thing," she called after him. "I've always had a vague memory of a letter coming that summer. After he got back. It was from Munich, a woman's name on the envelope in the corner."

Jack froze. He reached the door. "Oh yeah?"

"When I gave it to your father, he said it was from some old woman who owned the house he and his buddies roomed at for awhile. She wanted to see how he was doing back home in the States."

Jack turned to face his mother; it would've seemed strange not to. "Okay. Sounds reasonable." He reached for the doorknob. She'd never mentioned the damn letter before. How could she know anything?

She raised her penciled-on eyebrows. "Hmmm. Good thing I wasn't the suspicious type." She chuckled and gave Jack a quick hug, her familiar gardenia scent drifting about. "Talk soon, Jacky."

"Bye, Ma." He opened the door and escaped into warm sunshine, down the porch past the lilac bushes, happy to be in fresh air, free from skeletons hidden in cupboards and diaries.

CHAPTER 36

Several days later, as rain spit from the sky, Jack set plates of smoked Gouda cheese and Club crackers on the kitchen table. He'd sliced the cheese without slicing a finger and patted himself on the back for his choice of low-fat crackers. Guess Sherk was rubbing off on him.

After dumping a bag of Doritos into a large wooden bowl, he retrieved a carton of chunky salsa from the fridge and put it next to the orange chips. He surveyed the spread and looked at Boone. "As good as it gets. I'll just add a few napkins I swiped from Hans Biergarten, and we're all set."

Jenny and Tommy had planned to stop in for pre-dinner drinks after work, before heading to their respective houses. The occasion was the big reveal. Jack and his brother would tell their sister about their newly-discovered half-sister from Stuttgart. Although curious to see Jenny's reaction, he wasn't entirely comfortable with the impending conversation. Would she be upset? Another brother, Andy, was out of town, so Jack would inform him later. Mike, the youngest, lived in Denver supposedly; hard to tell when he would be available, if ever.

Jack had decided to let Jenny take the journal home and read it alone, but he'd tell her the general content, and Jack would show her the long-ago letter and snapshot first. Even though he enjoyed their company, he hoped she and Tommy wouldn't stay too long. Still not big on social occasions. Besides, the final season of *Breaking Bad* was now available for streaming. Another advantage of returning to Chicago.

Rain still pelted the windowpanes, and gloom edged its way through the blinds when the doorbell rang. Boone jumped into his usual frenzy as the door opened and Jenny walked inside.

"Honey, I'm home," she called out.

Jack met her in the entry. "Just leave the umbrella on the floor here."

"Got it. Hey, Boone." Jenny smoothed her damp wavy dark hair and set the umbrella down. "Damn, thought the rain would quit by now." She wiped her feet on the small area rug.

Jack took her shoulders and pressed her against him in a hug. "How's my favorite sister?"

She stepped back and looked at him, eyebrows pursed. "Who are you, and what have you done with my brother?"

"Always the comedian. Come on in and have some gourmet appetizers and a drink." He led her into the kitchen.

Jenny looked at the table. "I'm impressed, Jack. Who arranged the cheese slices?" She turned to open a cabinet door and took out three small plates.

"Oh yeah, forgot those. Can't remember everything." He opened the fridge and reached for a Sam Adams and a coke. He filled a glass with ice, then added the soda, and handed it to her.

"Thanks." Jenny took a plate and selected several cheese slices and crackers. "I'll leave the chips and dip for you and Tommy."

They settled in the living room with plates on the coffee table, drinks in hand. Jenny straightened the scarf around her neck, its red print contrasting with her black top and pants. A trim woman, whose sapphire eyes matched Jack's, she was six years younger than him, and had been the baby sister to three older brothers until Mike was born two years later. Yes, a typical Irish Catholic family, at least from the outside.

"Mom mentioned you had a nice lunch with her the other day." Jenny sipped her soda.

"Yeah, the usual meal fit for twenty people. The old gal seems as feisty as ever."

Jenny chuckled. "I didn't tell her I was coming here tonight. I just said I'd call you soon about Germany. I assumed she wasn't included."

"Right. Just a young kids' night."

"So, how was the trip?"

Jack took a drink. "Lots of history to take in. Nice digs at Sherk's summer house."

"Okay. What else? What about Dachau? Mom wanted you to—"

"I'll wait for Tommy. He knows some of it, but—"

As if on cue, the doorbell chimed; Boone barked and jumped at the door, greeting Tommy as he ambled in. "Well, the gang's all here." He bent down and tousled the big dog's furry neck.

Jenny finished chewing a cracker. "Go get your beer and snacks. Jack, or at least some gourmet imposter posing as Jack, spent all day preparing them."

"Grrr," came from Jack.

Tommy did as he was told and joined them in the living room. Jack noticed he glanced at Jenny's glass beside her. Apparently, she noticed too.

She took her glass, held it up. "Here, do you wanna sniff? It's coca cola, Tommy. Not dark beer."

"Sorry, Jen. Didn't mean to —"

"Right." She put the glass down. "It's just I've been doing so well, going to meetings, but I guess I'm supposed to appreciate your concern."

"Well, sorry anyway." Tommy leaned back. "Change of subject. Okay, what has Jack told you so far about Deutschland?"

"Nothing. For some odd reason he wanted to wait for you." She looked from one brother to the other. "What's the deal? Did you visit Dachau? Find out something about Dad?"

Jack shrugged and glanced at Tommy. "Where to begin?"

"Gradually," Tommy said.

"You're scaring me, guys." Jenny straightened. "What's going on?"

"Sorry," Jack said. "No need to be scared. First off, we tracked down a woman who met Pa during the war. More like the end of the war. But first you need to see the letter." He leaned over and opened a drawer of a nearby end table, then reached for a small envelope. Slowly removing the letter inside, he explained how he and Tommy had uncovered it in their father's box of war memorabilia.

Jenny's eyes widened as she stared at Jack, listening to the message in the letter.

"My God, Dad had a wartime romance. What about Mom? Did she ever know?" She brushed her hair back.

Tommy took a chip and dipped it in spicy red salsa. "Nah, I doubt it."

Jack said, "I thought that too until she said she remembered the letter and Pa telling her it was from an old German woman who owned his boarding house."

"You also told me on the phone she talked more about Pa's nightmares, how he called out names," Tommy added.

Jack coughed. "Anyway, Jenny, we're sure Ma's in the dark. So, it was Sherk who did the grunt work locating Ariana Gunther's nursing home in Weimar." Jack explained their trip to see Ariana, meeting her sister Renate instead, and listening to the family's story leading to the war years.

"Then we found out first hand how Pa met her." Jack retrieved the journal from the drawer and handed it to Jenny.

Tears welled up in her eyes as her hands caressed the leather cover. She opened it to the first page. "This is Daddy's handwriting, I can tell." She looked up at Jack. "When can I read it?"

Jack extended a paper napkin to Jenny, which prompted a surprised look from his sister before she took it and used it to dab a tear. Jack watched her and realized, perhaps for the first time, she had never completely understood the angst he and his brothers had harbored towards their father. After all, Jenny, who was younger and blessed with female blamelessness, had never borne the brunt of John Bailey's temper.

"You can take it home." Jack gently laid his hand on her arm. "But if the kids or Bob see it, tell 'em mum's the word. Gotta keep it from Ma."

"There are a few pages at the end Ariana wrote, in German of course," Tommy said. "Sometime Sherk can translate for you." He turned to Jack. "But, Jack, you remember the gist of it, right?"

Jack nodded before turning to open the drawer again. "Almost forgot. A picture of the two of them." He held out the worn snapshot to Jenny.

Gazing at the image of her father and Ariana, she placed her hand on her heart. "Wow. She was beautiful. Looked like a movie star from the old days."

"Ingrid Bergman?" Tommy said.

Jenny looked at him. "Yes, yes, she's the one." She handed the photo to Jack. "Can't absorb all this. Surreal."

Jack glanced at Tommy. "Now, is she ready for the next episode?"

Tommy shrugged. "Now or never."

"What the hell? There's more?" Jenny looked puzzled; eyebrows raised.

"I'll plunge right in." Jack took a swig. "Remember how you always begged Ma for a sister? Not fair you only had brothers?"

"Jack," Tommy said.

Jenny looked from one to the other. "What the fu — "

"Language." Jack's eyebrows met, forming a mock frown.

"Turns out you — we all have a half sister."

Jenny's mouth dropped. "What?" The word seemed to catch in her throat before escaping.

Jack leaned closer. "You're sitting there in shock, but yeah, Pa and Ariana. The girl was born after Pa came home. He never found out about her."

Jenny stood and aimlessly wandered to the kitchen table and back. "You mean, she — "

"Ariana married an old flame of hers who said he'd raise the girl as his own. Her name is Monika. We met her at Renate's when she stopped in to visit Ariana. She doesn't know about Pa at all."

Jenny sat on the sofa and furiously swatted invisible crumbs from her sleeve. She listened while Jack described the details, translations, and Monika herself. Of course, he left out the part about his initial attraction to Monika. This, he determined, was one secret only Sherk would ever be privy to.

"No picture of her?" Jenny looked hopeful.

"Sorry, no. But her profile looks like yours." Jack placed his hand on Jenny's chin, gently shifting its trajectory. "Same nose and chin."

"Jeez, really? I'd love to meet her. Oh, guys, maybe we can look her up some day?"

"Not gonna happen, Jen," Jack said. "She doesn't know Pa was her biological father. Renate doesn't wanna tell her."

"Why not?" A change came over Jenny. She stood, infuriated, her eyes darting between Jack and Tommy. "She has a right to know who her real father... What about her medical records? Lots of people are starting to search for their ancestors through DNA and — ."

Tommy stood and eased his sister back into her seat. "We can't tell anything, Jen. It's up to Renate to tell her."

"Why? She's only her aunt. Her mother isn't capable of it, but still." Hand trembling, Jenny drained her glass. Jack bet she wished for a vodka on ice about now.

He wiped his forehead. "I thought that way at first too, but it's Renate's place to tell her. We have no right horning in."

They sat in silence for a minute, Jack's and Tommy's eyes remaining on their sister as her breathing calmed. She fiddled with her hair. "I still can't wrap my head around it. Having a sister across the world. I could try and talk Bob into a trip to Germany in a couple years when we've paid off more of the kids' college loans."

Jack hadn't told his family, other than Tommy, about his windfall a few months ago. One of these days he would, and offer to help Jenny and the other kids with college funds. Meanwhile, he balked at the idea of Jenny traipsing off to Germany and hunting down Monika Gunther or whatever her name might be.

Tommy said, "Let it settle, Jen. See how you feel in a few days." Then, as though speaking to a child, "I think you should stay away from Ma for a week so you don't slip and bring up anything."

Jenny rolled her eyes. "Christ, Tom, gimme a little credit. I'm not gonna blab to anyone." She turned to Jack. "But how 'bout Andy and Mike? Are you gonna tell them?"

"Sometime," Jack said. "Andy soon. Mike? Who cares?" The black sheep of the Bailey family, Mike hadn't communicated in years and lived in Denver, Pittsburgh, or Timbuktu as far as they knew.

Glancing at her watch, Jenny picked up her plate and glass and made her way into the kitchen.

"Gotta run. I'll take the diary, read it tonight." She gathered her purse and journal together while Jack folded her umbrella and handed it to her. Again, she looked at him as though he'd dropped from outer space. "I must admit, Jack, you seem different somehow. Who are you?"

"What do you mean? I'm not an asshole anymore?"

Jenny squinted at him. "Not as big a one. Just a little softer."

"Hell, not me. Never happen." But Jack recognized his Germany experience had changed him. Apparently, others would see it too. A strange warmth rose within him. What was it? Benevolence? Compassion? Jack tried to fight the emotions, but his efforts were thwarted by his sister's curious expression.

Jack avoided her eyes. "At least it quit raining," he said, glancing at Tommy. "Wanna stay?"

Tommy stood. "Thanks, but I need to run too."

The three half-hugged one another, and said their goodbyes, promising to get together soon. Would Jenny forget her desire to meet Monika? He would check with her in a few days.

Meanwhile, Jack needed to get in gear and follow up on plans. Plans for the rest of his life.

CHAPTER 37
Five weeks later

The party was in full swing when Jack arrived at Tommy's house on a warm, humid afternoon in August. Not as bad as Texas, but Chicago had its share of summer heat. Tommy lived in Oak Forest, twenty miles south of Bridgeport, in a two-story red brick house with a spacious front yard surrounded by trees from next-door yards. Thick, overhanging branches provided a sense of privacy and woodsy seclusion.

Until now, Jack had viewed his mother's birthday celebration as a dreaded duty. Gathering at her house or Tommy's to grill outdoors in the August heat, kids and grandkids running around, yammering away, not fun. Especially Jenny's daughter, Cate, born a few months earlier than his Elizabeth. Seeing Cate through the years had pierced his heart like a knife. Elizabeth would now be making college plans if only —. But today was different somehow. Driving the fifteen minutes from his house, he actually looked forward to Ma's birthday event. Well, not exactly, but at least he was fine with the idea. Perhaps Jenny was right; could he be getting soft?

Several parked cars packed the driveway, so he slid the Beemer along Le Claire Avenue across from thick trees and high bushes on the other side of the street.

He walked up the driveway. A short sidewalk curved its way to the porch lined with black iron urns spilling over with red geraniums with trailing vines. They reminded Jack of the anemones in German gardens.

He walked in the front door, sounds of laughter and chatter ringing in the air. A scent of smoked beef wafted through the room.

"Hey, where's the food?" Jack called as heads turned towards him. An appropriate way to announce my arrival, he thought.

Erica, Sherk's wife, sat on the sofa talking to Jenny. Jack strolled towards them. "Erica, good to see you. How are you?" Not a question

145

for a cancer patient, but he hoped she wouldn't take offense. Hopefully, she'd cut him some slack.

"Hi, Jack." She held her hand up to touch his. "I'm feeling better every day. Things seem to be working out."

"Hey, great news." He couldn't help noticing her gaunt face and arms, but she should gain her weight back soon. Still, a glimpse of a red flag flashed in his mind.

"I'm glad you had an interesting time in Munich," she said. "Jenny was telling me a little about it. Of course, Sherk gave me a report too."

"Yeah, a great trip." He wondered how much Sherk had told her.

"Drinks are in the kitchen, usual place." Jenny said.

"Trying to get rid of me?"

"Always, Jack." She turned her attention back to Erica.

He greeted Sherk and Jenny's husband, Bob, who stood across the room chatting and drinking beer.

Jack patted Sherk's shoulder. "Gotta grab a beer. Don't go away."

He made his way through the tidy living room, decorated in traditional style, with burgundy brocade upholstered chairs and sofa, framed landscape pictures, and an Audubon blue heron print above the fireplace mantle.

"Jacky, there you are. About time," Maureen exclaimed as Jack walked into the kitchen. "Tommy's about done grilling."

"Hey, Ma. Happy Birthday." He embraced his mother, catching a whiff of gardenia.

He turned to Tommy's wife, and with a quick embrace said, "Hi, Mary. Good to see ya."

"Hello, Jack. I'm sure you had a good time testing out all the German beer." She wiped her hands on a dish towel.

"Jawohl," He raised his brows and nodded, mocking how he'd impressed himself. "Even picked up some German language, meine Frau." Jack took a can of Old Style from the fridge and popped the lid.

Mary said, "Tommy's in the back waiting for your help manning the grill."

She and Maureen chattered like birds, placing bowls of potato salad, baked beans covered with bacon strips, hamburger buns, and other items on the large circular kitchen table that would serve as a buffet. French doors led to a flagstone patio with a picnic table and an additional round table and deck chairs nearby.

Outside, Tommy, master of his domain, stood over the gas grill merging meat and fire as only a true American backyard chef could. For months now, Jack couldn't help but draw comparisons between American and European ways of life. His mouth twitched. What the hell had happened to him? Along with his newfound sensitivity, he'd also apparently become culturally aware.

Trees and shrubs surrounded the back, creating a makeshift boundary from neighboring yards. Blue and purple hydrangeas still bloomed, along with several shrub roses. Hosta foliage filled in, leaving no empty beds. Mary and Maureen were the family gardeners.

"Master chef at work I see." Jack closed the glass door behind him. "Kinda hot for grilling."

"Not bad with two fans going." Tommy looked up. "Got the ceiling fan, and one on the other side of the picnic table."

Jack peered under the grill's hood. "Whatcha got there?"

Tommy flipped over a burger with a long-handled spatula. He turned to Jack. "In honor of your trip, we got bratwurst. Hot dogs and hamburgers for the grandkids or anyone else who doesn't appreciate German cuisine."

After placing the spatula on the grill tray, he lifted a sheet of aluminum foil from a platter, grabbed a pair of tongs, and transferred the sausages to the grill. "Best way to cook bratwurst, Jack. Gotta parboil 'em in beer so they're cooked through, then grill to get the outsides brown and crisp."

Jack shook his head. "I'll see if they're as good as we had at the Hofbräuhaus." Jack envied Tommy's relationship with his kids and grandkids. His chef's apron, along with a few smudges of barbeque sauce, displayed an image of a spatula above the words, 'Our dad is flipping awesome.' A far cry from their pa.

He watched Tommy's small grandsons tossing a Frisbee back and forth. Guess he'd never experience grandchildren. Don't dwell on it, he ordered himself.

Fifteen minutes later, everyone was sitting at the two tables, eating and talking. They had filled their plates at the kitchen table and brought them outside to sit on the patio. Tommy stood ready to serve their meat of choice. "Ma, now you can finally sit down and chill."

Maureen had insisted on bringing potato salad and rather than relaxing with the others in the living room, had putzed around in the kitchen.

Mary had told her earlier, "Come on, Maureen. Jenny and I will get everything ready," You go and sit with your guests."

"Oh, no. I want to help in the kitchen as long as I'm able." She brushed her red curls from her cheek.

Jenny said, "Yeah, the real reason is, she doesn't trust us to set up things the right way."

"Oh, go on with you." Maureen had proceeded to rearrange the silverware and dishes on the buffet table.

· · · · ·

Sherk paused and put his fork down. "Tommy, this bratwurst is second to none. Sehr gut."

"Yeah, gotta admit its almost up to Munich standards." Jack leaned toward the little boys stuffing hot dogs and burgers in their mouths. "Hey, Ethan, don't you wanna try a good German sausage?"

The boy hesitated, his tufty brown hair in his eyes. "No thanks, Uncle Jack. Maybe when I grow up."

"Yeah," Liam chimed in. "When we're old like you and Grandpa." He and Ethan snickered, seemingly proud of the joke.

Maureen chuckled and took a sip of red wine. "Boys, you be nice to your elders. Besides, if you think they're old—"

"Ha, Gran, you're the oldest one here," Ethan said. "Grandpa said he hoped the house wouldn't burn down from all—"

"Hush, Ethan," Mary scolded. "Mind what you're doing. You just dribbled ketchup on your new shirt. Your mom won't be happy." Tommy's and Mary's daughter and son-in-law were away for a long weekend.

And so, the chatter carried on amongst old and young alike. Jack noticed Erica ate less than half a burger and picked at the potato salad. She winced occasionally, obviously in discomfort. Still, she was a trooper, chatting and smiling as though all was right with her world. Jack wondered if Sherk had told her about the journal and their sister no one realized existed. No matter. As long as Ma was in the dark.

· · · · ·

"Who's ready for cake and ice cream?" Tommy called.

"We are, we are" yelled the little boys.

Maureen stood. "Let's clear the tables and wait a while. I'm too full now." She ruffled Liam's hair.

The rest acquiesced as they carried their dishes inside to the kitchen.

"Ma, go in the living room, talk to Erica and Jenny," Tommy said. "Mary and I will clean up here and Jack will do the grill."

"Huh?" Jack said. "Rather do kitchen duty." Didn't want to admit he never learned how to grill, nor had he wanted to. Besides, "kitchen duty" would give him a chance to talk to Mary. See if Tommy had told her about the journal and their new sister.

"My brother volunteering to do dishes." Tommy turned to the others and joked, "I told you Germany had softened him." Then to Jack: "Go ahead and help in here. Oh, and in case you're wondering, the dishwasher is that contraption you pull open next to the sink." Having triumphed with a final jab, Tommy smiled and picked up the grill brush.

Chapter 38

After Maureen was shooed into the living room and Tommy headed for the patio with the boys to clean the grill, Jack helped put silverware and dishes around the sink while Mary loaded the dishwasher.

She turned to Jack. "Her brown eyes glinted. She straightened her sleeveless tan print top. A woman substantial in size, she was forever trying the latest diets, to no avail, as she'd sigh.

"I want to thank you for going to Germany and finding out about the letter, and more about John."

Surprised by her comment, he didn't need to worry about hinting around. She came right out with it. He put the empty potato salad bowl in the sink. "Oh, sure. Guess Tommy told you all about the situation."

"Yes, he did, Jack." She lowered her voice, glancing toward the living room. "In fact, he mentioned finding the letter, and later when you were in Munich, told me about this woman, Ariana, and the journal."

Jack nodded. "Good. Glad he did. Anything else?"

Mary hesitated. "About your half-sister. Yeah, that too."

Again, Jack said, "Good. You should be aware."

"The information seemed to do Tommy a world of good. I can tell he's a different person. I know it sounds very dramatic, but —" her voice trailed off as she put a glass in the dishwasher. "He doesn't fly off the handle when he forgets milk at Jewel-Osco anymore."

"That's great, Mary. I was hoping he'd change somehow after realizing all the crap Pa went through."

"He has changed, Jack, and in some way, he's forgiven John after all these years." Mary absently rinsed a bowl. "Jenny's doing fine too, Tommy tells me."

"Yeah, thank God. We're probably both remembering about nine, ten years ago at another birthday party for Ma when Jenny called – Well, when she'd clearly had too much. That time convinced Ma that yes, Jenny had a problem." Jack grimaced. "But now she's coming up on one year since the last slip."

Mary put her hand on Jack's arm. "Right, good for her. Ironic. I always thought it would've been you or Tommy who'd have the problem. You know, both cops like your dad."

"I agree."

Tommy and the boys interrupted the conversation as they came blundering into the kitchen. "You guys go upstairs." Tommy hustled them away. "Call you for dessert."

The boys scampered off, no doubt eager to play with their iPads or whatever the hell kids amused themselves with these days.

Mary turned. "Now that you're here, I'll relieve Jack and turn over dish duty to you."

"Yes, Ma'am." Tommy gave a mock salute.

Jack joined Sherk and Bob, who sat by the fireplace. "Sherk was just talking about your visit with his grandpa's family," Bob said. "I'm amazed he survived Stalingrad."

Jack sat in a chair beside him. "Yeah, great people. Changed my outlook on Germans."

Bob suppressed a cough. "I'm sure. Now Jenny's after me to go over there some summer. Could take the kids."

Jack stiffened, hoping Bob wouldn't notice. She probably had told her husband about Monika, and wanting to meet her. "Lots of good things to see there," was all Jack wanted to utter.

Sherk crossed his lanky legs. "It would be a wonderful education for the kids. Germany is full of history and culture, as you know."

Just then, the front door opened and a young, light-haired girl burst in. "Too late for dinner?" she called to no one in particular.

"Cate, you showed up." Jenny stood, smiling at her daughter. "Come sit by your grandma."

"Yes, come here, Caty bird," Maureen called out. "I've missed you."

Cate giggled and sashayed to the sofa, her long pony tail swinging. She wore a black, sleeveless top and white shorts showcasing long, thin legs.

"Happy Birthday, Grandma," she sat down and hugged Maureen. "You look beautiful."

"Ah, my favorite grandchild." Maureen planted a kiss on Cate's cheek.

It had become easier for Jack to be around Cate in the past couple years. She was seventeen, the age Elizabeth would be. As cousins, Elizabeth and Cate had often played together, dabbling in a fantasy world reserved for little girls. For a long time after Elizabeth and Karen were killed, Jack stayed away from Jenny's family. The pain was too intense, but the passage of time had helped ease his grief.

Cate was introduced to Erica, but had met Sherk before. "Awesome. I want to visit Germany. Mom agreed maybe we can go when I'm in college."

"See what you started, Jack?" Tommy appeared from the kitchen. "Now everyone wants to go, including Ma."

Maureen scoffed. "Not for me, Mister. The Ireland trip years ago was wonderful, but I'm too old for that now."

"Speaking of old ladies, are we ready for cake?" Jack said.

"Always the smart one, Jacky is." Maureen patted Cate's knee. "At least your other uncle respects me."

"Yay for Uncle Tommy," Cate said.

Several minutes later, everyone stood around the dining room table where two candles shaped like an eight and a seven flickered atop a three-layer cake adorned with candied pink roses and white icing.

Everyone sang the happy birthday song, some more in tune than others.

"Eww, that sounded terrible," Ethan groaned.

"Out of the mouths of brats." Tommy jostled the boy.

Jack held up a half full glass of beer. "Here's to Maureen O'Leary Bailey. May the good Lord take a liking to you…. but not too soon."

"Here, here," rang through the air.

"Speech, Ma," said Tommy, immediately joined by a chorus of "Yay, speech."

Maureen, flushed, dabbed at her eyes. "I won't get all mushy, but you all know how I care deeply about you. I say this every year, but this time we have our special guests, Erica and Sherk, so this Irish blessing has a special meaning."

She cleared her throat. "May joy and peace surround you, contentment latch your door, and happiness be with you now, and bless you evermore!"

Jack thought he saw tears welling in Erica's eyes. She looked up at Sherk and gazed. He took her hand. Was he choking up? No sooner had Jack raised this question, then something caught in his own throat.

Sherk gave a cough and placed his other hand in Maureen's. "And this is a German wish for you." He looked down on her shining face. "Ich wünsche dir zu deinem Geburtstag alles Liebe und Güte— verbringe einen wunderschönen Tag im Kreise deiner Lieben."

He glanced at everyone around the table. "Just in case you didn't get all that, I said that I wish you all the best on your birthday. May you spend a wonderful day surrounded by those you love."

Various "oohs" and "aahs" came from the group.

Maureen's lips quivered as she gave Sherk a hug. "Oh, Sherk, thank you so much. And for taking Jacky with you to your home across the ocean. It did him a lot of good. He's not quite as ornery as before." She raised her eyebrows at Jack. "I do believe he's getting a little soft."

"Aw, Ma, hate to disappoint you, but that'll never happen." He brushed his hair from his forehead. "Gotta admit Germany did me good, though. And you're almost as good a cook as Sherk's grandma."

"Oh, go on with you. Let's have cake," Maureen playfully shooed him off with a wave of her hand. "Hand me the cutter, Jenny. I'll slice the first piece."

Tommy said, "Okay everyone, you know the drill. Help yourself to cake. If you want ice cream, Cate will dish it out for you in the kitchen."

"I will?" she said. "That's what I get for being late."

"That's right, kid." Tommy turned to Maureen. "We have Kemp's Old-Fashioned Vanilla. Nothing but the best for our ma."

Maureen looked at Sherk and Erica. "Don't let my boys fool you. Once a year they're nice to me. And sometimes at Christmas."

Erica's eyes sparkled. "You have a lovely family, Maureen."

Highly debatable, Jack thought. But then again, perhaps they weren't so bad after all.

•   •   •   •   •

The rooms still buzzed with chatter and merriment as people lingered over their empty cake plates and coffee cups. Folks were scattered throughout the house, some in the living room, kitchen, patio. Jack wandered into the kitchen and noticed the little boys in the backyard, miniature Chicago Cubs, gleefully swinging plastic bats at wiffleballs pitched to them by Bob. Jack stood at the window, lost in the scene.

He thought again how he used to dislike family gatherings. Christmas and birthdays, more painful. But now, a sense of contentment filled his spirit, a forgotten sense, absent for many years. He'd gained a renewed gratitude for this family of his, with their flaws along with their strengths. However, he still was not complete, as if he were missing an appendage these past twelve years. But maybe the gap was shrinking. Perhaps he could live a meaningful life without a wife and children?

"Sneaking more ice cream?" His brother's voice roused him back from his thoughts. Tommy came and stood beside Jack at the window.

Jack turned. "Nah, just woolgathering."

"Bad sign, bro. How 'bout I grab Sherk and we walk down to the corner. Wear off some calories?"

"Sure." Jack followed Tommy into the living room.

"We're gonna rescue you from these women," Jack said to Sherk. "Let's take a short walk."

Sherk looked at Erica as if to gain her permission. She nodded. "Go ahead, honey. After that, we'll need to be on our way."

"We won't be gone long," Jack said as they walked out the door into the sunshine.

"Nice neighborhood, Tommy," Sherk said. "Some of the trees and flowers remind me of Munich."

The three men strolled in silence for a minute or two. Birds sang, and everything smelled fresh and green.

"It's been a good day, guys," Sherk said as he kicked a pebble into the grass. "Thanks for inviting us."

"Yeah, Ma insisted," Jack said, then something inside prompted him to add, "but I wanted you here too. You're absolutely part of the family."

"You're stuck with us now," Tommy added. "But your trip was good for me too, the end result anyway. I've been almost able to let the old man go. To figure out—" He paused, gathering himself. "To finally get what probably caused his demons. Go on with things." He shook his head, looked pointedly at Jack. "I'm damn lucky Mary's put up with me all these years."

Jack recalled the time, decades ago, when Mary walked out with the kids. Said Tommy had a month to straighten out, or she'd call it quits. He shaped up in a hurry.

They turned the corner and ambled along the sidewalk. An older man approached them walking his German Shepherd. When the gap between them bridged, Jack smiled. "Nice dog."

The man returned the smile. "Thanks. He just turned five." He kept walking.

"Well, perhaps you can put the journal and the war, and even Monika behind you, and be happy in what you have, namely your family." Sherk, ever the wise one.

Jack thought for a few seconds. "Yeah, let's hope Jenny doesn't get any ideas about tracking down Monika if and when she goes over there."

But he agreed Sherk was right about leaving the past behind. Ariana's story had tapped into the recesses of his mind and reached undiscovered places. On a broader scale, his awareness had become sharper of people coping in times of turmoil, beyond their control. He thought of his pa's buddy, Bill, who had seen the weak become strong, and the strong become weak. Could something like the Third Reich happen again? In America?

Jack suppressed that thought, and instead, thought of his family. A family bonded by secrets. Right or wrong? Not for Jack to decide. For now, for the first time, he treasured the love generated by this family, these folks who would always be on his side. He was getting soft, but that was okay. At last.

•   •   •   •   •

And all because of a letter composed decades ago, written by someone far removed from them, but who had gently filtered her way into their lives. Some for better, some for worse.

•   •   •   •   •

A girl on a bike pedaled by, braids flying in the breeze. Jack thought she's lucky to live in this time of peace. He hoped she'd stay safe.

He stepped over a crack on the sidewalk. "Did I tell you guys I'm gonna meet with the director of the Citizens for Animal Sanctuary?" Jack knew damn well he hadn't told them. Hadn't told anyone.

"No," Tommy said. "About expanding it?"

"Yeah. Gotta do something worthwhile." Jack hoped his idea would fly. He had the means now to add two new wings to the shelter. In memory of Karen and Elizabeth.

"Jack, you're on a roll," Sherk said. "As I said once before, 'Hope is the thing with feathers.'"

Jack stopped and pointed to a tree. "And I see a bluebird."

He didn't, but it sounded good.

ABOUT THE AUTHOR

Meg Lelvis grew up in northern Minnesota and taught English and psychology in Houston and Dallas. Her fiction and poetry have won awards from Houston Writers Guild and Houston Writers House. Her first novel, *Bailey's Law,* won the 2017 Maxy Award for best mystery. Meg's second Bailey novel, *Blind Eye,* won Maxy Award's second place for best mystery in 2018.

A Letter from Munich is her third novel. Meg resides in Houston with her husband and two dogs.

NOTE FROM THE AUTHOR

Word-of-mouth is crucial for any author to succeed. If you enjoyed the book, please leave a review online—anywhere you are able. Even if it's just a sentence or two. It would make all the difference and would be very much appreciated.

Thanks!
Meg

Thank you so much for reading one of **Meg Lelvis's** novels.
If you enjoyed the experience, please check out our
recommended title for your next great read!

Bailey's Law by Meg Lelvis

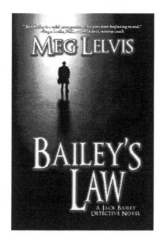

"An intelligent, immersive police procedural that will leave you pining
for another Jack Bailey novel."
–BEST THRILLERS

Made in the USA
Middletown, DE
20 September 2023

38851252R00102